**Other books by
Ann M. Martin**

Rachel Parker, Kindergarten Show-off
Eleven Kids, One Summer
Ma and Pa Dracula
Yours Turly, Shirley
Ten Kids, No Pets
Slam Book
Just a Summer Romance
Missing Since Monday
With You and Without You
Me and Katie (the Pest)
Stage Fright
Inside Out
Bummer Summer

BABY-SITTERS LITTLE SISTER series
THE BABY-SITTERS CLUB mysteries
THE BABY-SITTERS CLUB series

MARY ANNE AND THE LITTLE PRINCESS

Ann M. Martin

AN
APPLE
PAPERBACK

SCHOLASTIC INC.
New York Toronto London Auckland Sydney

Cover art by Hodges Soileau

ISBN 0-590-69208-9

12 11 10 9 8 7 6 5 4 3 2 1   6 7 8 9/9 0 1/0

Printed in the U.S.A.   40

First Scholastic printing, November 1996

*The author gratefully acknowledges
Peter Lerangis
for his help in
preparing this manuscript.*

Many thanks to
David McMullen

MARY ANNE AND THE LITTLE PRINCESS

CHAPTER 1

"When I say 'Hut,' " Logan Bruno announced, "Kristy hikes the football to me and goes long. I fake a handoff to Hannie, Linny flags right, and David Michael does a quick button hook. Okay?"

"Right!" shouted Kristy Thomas.

"Yyyes!" cried Linny Papadakis.

"Okay," said Hannie Papadakis.

"What's a button hook?" asked David Michael Thomas.

Good question, I thought.

I didn't really hear the answer, although I know it had something to do with running and catching. To tell you the truth, the moment Logan started explaining, my attention snapped back to the novel I was reading, *Catherine, Called Birdy*.

We were spending a Sunday morning at Kristy's house. Who are "we"? Well, I'm Mary Anne Spier. Kristy is my all-time best friend, and Logan is my boyfriend. I love them dearly, but as soon as they'd started playing football with Kristy's little brother and the two Papadakis kids, I'd excused myself.

Sitting against a maple tree with my novel, bundled in my wool jacket, I was perfectly happy. I figured I'd read a few chapters before my stepmom picked me up. She was late, but that's sort of her style.

Do you think it's weird to be reading outdoors on a chilly November day? I don't. I just love books. Besides, I had no other choice. Playing football is bad enough. Playing with Logan is downright frightening. He happens to be on the Stoneybrook Middle School football team, and he throws extremely hard.

Kristy doesn't mind. She's a great athlete. The kids don't mind either, because they think Logan's a superstar. And he does throw very gently to them. (David Michael and Hannie are seven, and Linny's nine.)

I've tried playing. Logan has explained the rules to me a million times. Kristy insists that it's easy and fun. But it's not. The moment I see a football headed in my direction, I can think of only one thing to do.

Duck.

So, on fall weekends, I always carry a paperback with me. It comes in handy whenever pigskin fever strikes.

Pigskin fever seemed to have struck my hometown, Stoneybrook, Connecticut. The SMS Chargers were undefeated. Logan told me they were "assured of a playoff berth." At first I thought he meant "birth" and I was totally confused. But he explained that the team was going to be in the district championships, which apparently is a very nice thing.

Why is someone like me attracted to such athletic people? I have no idea. My dad says I take after him. He's terrible at sports, too, but his best friends at his law firm are athletic. In fact, Dad once told me that my mom played on her college basketball team.

When I say "my mom," I mean my birth mom. As much as I love my stepmom, I call her by her first name, Sharon.

If a genie appeared and granted me one wish, you know what it would be? To go into the past and meet my mother. You see, she died when I was a baby. Do you think it's possible to miss someone you don't remember? I do. My dad doesn't talk about her much, but I know he was devastated when she died — so devastated that he had to let my grandparents take care of me while he grieved.

When Dad took me back, he felt kind of overwhelmed by single parenthood. He decided to be Mr. Strict. I had to wear superconservative clothes and keep my hair in pigtails right through seventh grade. I had to go to bed earlier than some nine-year-olds I knew.

Don't worry, things have changed. I'm in eighth grade now. I'm thirteen years old, I have a reasonable curfew, and no, I do not look like Pippi Longstocking anymore. Dad finally realized I was growing up. He's been a lot happier himself, too, especially after meeting Sharon.

Actually, *meeting* isn't the right word. *Remeeting* is more like it. Dad and Sharon were sweethearts at Stoneybrook High School. They broke up, though, because Sharon's parents looked down their noses at my dad. (Hmmph.) Sharon went off to California, taking Dad's heart with her. Well, temporarily. He did meet my mom soon after. Anyway, Dad and Sharon completely lost touch. (Now, if this were a movie, you'd see the words *Many years later* . . . on the screen.) Cut to my seventh-grade year. I made friends with a girl named Dawn Schafer who had just moved to Stoneybrook from California, with her younger brother and her divorced mom. (Suspenseful music here.) It took us awhile to realize her mom was *the* Sharon in Dad's romantic past.

Have you ever seen *Fiddler on the Roof?* In it, this character named Yente is constantly trying to match couples in marriage. Well, Dawn and I were double Yentes. Dad and Sharon didn't have a chance. Before long, wedding bells were ringing. Suddenly I had a great stepmom, a great stepsister, and a great new house (Dad and I moved into Sharon's two-hundred-year-old farmhouse).

Unfortunately, Dawn doesn't live there anymore. At least not full-time. She moved back to California to live with her dad. (Her younger brother, Jeff, had done the same thing earlier on.) It wasn't that they hated Stoneybrook or anything. They were just terribly homesick.

I miss Dawn so much. But I don't want to dwell on that. I'll just cry.

That's another thing you should know about me. I cry a lot. I cry when I'm happy and when I'm upset. Sad movies are the worst. Last Christmas I invited Kristy over to watch *It's a Wonderful Life*, and she brought along an umbrella. Logan says I have an obscure condition called Spier's Tears.

Aside from the crying, I'm a pretty average person, I guess. I'm just over five feet tall. I have short brown hair and brown eyes. My friends call my wardrobe "preppy," but I think of it as neat and not too flashy. They also call me shy and sensitive, but I think that's because I happen to enjoy listening to people.

I looked at my watch and did a double take. It was almost noon. Sharon was supposed to have picked me up at eleven. As I mentioned, she's not exactly the promptest person in the world, but this was unusual.

"And he fumbles the ball, right into the bleachers!" Logan's voice boomed out.

Before I could look up, the football was tumbling across my paperback.

A moment later, Logan and Kristy were tumbling over me. Linny, Hannie, and David Michael followed. (Catherine, called Birdy, flew silently toward the sidewalk.)

David Michael grabbed the ball. "Don't let Logan have it!" he screamed.

"Oh, yeah?" Logan said, tickling him.

Laughing, David Michael handed the ball to Hannie, who gave it to me.

I tried to hand it to Logan, but I was buried under a pile of kids.

VRRRRROOOM!

We all looked out to the street. A moving van was lumbering by. On its side were the words *Worldwide Moving — From Airport to Homeport*.

On another street, you might not notice something like that. But McLelland Road never has much traffic. It's hilly and curvy and lined with enormous houses and huge yards.

The truck pulled to a stop halfway down the block.

"Who's moving in?" Linny asked.

Kristy shrugged. "I don't know. I haven't seen any *For Sale* signs."

Two men and a woman in work clothes hopped out of the cab. We watched them go around to the back of the van and open it.

One of the first things they took out was an enormous Madeline doll.

"Kids!" Hannie squealed.

"Girls," Linny groaned.

Kristy's face lit up. "Clients."

I should explain. Kristy, Logan, and I belong to a group called the Baby-sitters Club, or BSC. Kristy's the president. She's also our number one business rustler-upper. You should see her in a mall. Whenever she spots an unfamiliar family with small children — *zoom* — she's on top of them with a smile, a handshake, and a BSC flier.

She began digging into her jeans pocket.

"Kristy, you're not — " Logan began.

"Got one!" Kristy said triumphantly, pulling out a crumpled, sweat-soaked sheet of paper.

Before anyone could say a word, Kristy was sprinting down McLelland Road, toward the van.

"She's possessed," Logan muttered.

I tucked the football under one arm, picked up my book with the other, and followed everybody else down the street.

By the time we all caught up to Kristy, she had cornered one of the moving guys. He was holding the flier, looking at it as though it were written in ancient Urdu.

"And we have a special introductory offer," Kristy was saying. "An hour free with the first job, and a money-back guarantee."

"Well, uh, I don't have kids," the guy replied.

"It's not for you," Kristy said. "Please leave it for the family that's moving in. You don't know their names, do you?"

The man peeked into the truck and checked a packing label. "Kent."

Linny raised his eyebrows. "Like, Clark?"

"That's Superman," David Michael said.

"Superman's moving into this house?" Hannie asked.

Linny let out a deep, exasperated breath. "Superman doesn't have a Madeline doll."

"Maybe he has a daughter," Logan suggested.

"We'll have to charge extra," Kristy said. "We've never had to sit for a kid who could fly."

I watched the moving guy trudge up a long

flagstone pathway. That was when I really noticed the house.

Well, I *assumed* it was a house. It could have been an institute or a museum or something. It was enormous, with ivy-covered brick walls and at least four chimneys. A wing extended diagonally out from the left side, with bay windows that overlooked a huge side yard.

The movers unloaded a dark wooden writing desk, a doll house, a girl's bike, and tons of boxes.

"Don't they use furniture?" Logan asked.

"Maybe they can't afford it," Hannie suggested.

"Does Superman get paid?" David Michael asked.

"You know, I never saw anyone move out of this house," Kristy remarked. "I thought the Atkinsons still lived here."

"Maybe these people are just house-sitting," I said, "or renting."

Kristy shrugged. "Could be. Mr. and Mrs. Atkinson travel a lot."

The three kids were all trying to peek into the van, giggling and whispering about Superman.

"Come on, guys, our time-out's almost up," Logan said, trotting back toward the house. "Mary Anne, toss it!"

Oh, great. He was going to force me to make a fool of myself. I tried to fit my fingers around the football.

Honk honk!

I turned toward the street. Sharon's car pulled up to the curb. I tucked the football back under my arm, and boy, was I grateful.

Sharon leaned across the front seat and rolled down the passenger window. With a sheepish grin, she called out, "Hi! Sorry I'm late, Mary Anne."

"Hi, Sharon," said Logan and Kristy, running up behind me.

"Is everything all right?" I asked,

"Yes," Sharon replied. "I was working on my computer, and I'd forgotten to set its clock to Eastern Standard Time."

Kristy gave her a Look. "The time change happened a week ago."

"Well, at least I did all the regular clocks in the house." Sharon sighed. "I just couldn't believe how much time I had on my hands."

"Oh," said Kristy.

Typical Sharon, I knew she was thinking.

Sharon can be a little absentminded. In our house, it's not unusual to find the tennis balls in the dishwasher, or her credit cards in the laundry detergent box. Luckily my dad is an excellent cook, or we'd all have to develop a taste for salad sprinkled with cinnamon, or shell pasta with watermelon slices (yes, she actually did that once).

I noticed then that Sharon was staring at my upper body strangely. "Mary Anne, are you . . . ?"

I realized I was still holding the football. "Oh, this? Well, um, I was just — "

"You should see her play," Logan butted in. "A total natural. She and Kristy are going to form a football team like the Krushers."

"Really?" piped up Linny the Eavesdropper.

"Mary Anne's Marauders," Logan replied.

"Manglers," Kristy suggested.

I felt myself blush. I threw the football toward Logan and hopped into the car.

As I waved good-bye, Sharon started driving away. "This is a side of you I've never seen, Mary Anne," she said.

I couldn't help laughing. "Me neither."

CHAPTER 2

"Being stupid is bad enough," said Claudia Kishi, munching on a pretzel nugget. "But being humongous and stupid is worse."

"You're not humongous," Kristy spoke up. "Would you pass me some of those?"

"You're not stupid, either," I added.

"Thanks, Mary Anne. Can we do homework together at your house tonight?"

"Sure," I replied.

"I'm starving!" cried Jessica Ramsey.

"Feed me, feed me," said Abby Stevenson.

Jessi, Kristy, Abby, Mallory Pike, and Stacey McGill all sat forward expectantly. They looked like baby birds in a nest.

Our Friday BSC meeting was about to begin. We were gathered in Claudia's bedroom, our official headquarters, doing our favorite things: chatting and eating.

And complaining. Unfortunately, Claudia had to repeat seventh grade this year, and she

12

was having adjustment problems. "None of you know what it's like to be left back," Claudia said, tossing little bags of pretzel nuggets around the room. "I mean, okay, I understand my classes finally, and that's good. But half the time I ask myself, 'What was so hard about this the first time?' Then I tell myself not to worry about that. *Then* I look around, and I notice everyone's so much smaller than me. I'm huge. I feel like Alice in Wonderland or something. You know, until this year I used to think that was a person's name — you know, Alison Wonderland? Ha. But now I know better. So I guess I must be getting smarter this year, huh?"

Abby leaned toward me. "Did you understand that?"

Whack! Kristy slammed a plastic hammer on Claudia's desk. "This meeting of the Baby-sitters Club shall come to order!"

"Ow! My ears!" Jessi said.

"*Shall?*" Mallory asked.

"What's the difference between *shall* and *will?*" Claudia asked.

"I think one's feminine and the other's short for William," Abby replied.

Claudia gave her a Look. "And *I'm* the one who was left back?"

You may have the impression that we're all a little crazy. Actually, we're best friends, and we just feel comfortable around each other.

How does the club work? The idea is simple. We meet Mondays, Wednesdays, and Fridays from five-thirty to six. We use Claudia's room, because she's the only club member who has a private phone line. Clients call us during business hours to request sitting jobs. They like the fact that they need to make only one call, and we like the fact that we have steady work.

Well, most of the time we do. Sometimes the commitment can be exhausting. We even split up for awhile, because the club seemed to be taking over our lives. You know what? We couldn't stay apart. We all love baby-sitting too much. Not to mention the fact that our clients and charges were upset. We decided to start up again, giving ourselves a probationary period, just in case.

That Friday, our probationary period had officially ended — and we had unanimously decided to be a real club again! That was the main reason we were so happy.

"Any new business?" Kristy began, then immediately barged on: "Glad I asked. Client alert! I saw the new family in my neighborhood today, the Kents."

"Clark and Lois?" Jessi said.

"What are they like?" Mallory asked.

"Well, at first it was hard to see them

14

through the dark glass of their chauffeured limo," Kristy replied.

"Excuuuse me," Stacey said.

"But I watched them leave the car and go inside," Kristy continued. "A girl and her dad and mom. She looks about eight or nine."

"The mom?" Claudia asked.

Kristy scowled at her. "Very funny. Anyway, I gave the dad our flier. He was really nice and he said they'd seen the other ones."

"Ones?" I asked.

"I've been putting one in their mailbox every day," Kristy replied.

Abby cracked up. "That's subtle."

Kristy threw an empty pretzel nuggets bag at her.

Kristy, in case you haven't noticed, has a very strong personality. She runs meetings with an iron hand, and doesn't tolerate unexcused lateness or absence. We're all used to her, but sometimes she can be bossy and overbearing. She doesn't mean to be like that. She was just born that way. I should know. She used to rearrange my blocks when we were babies. (I don't actually remember this, but my dad insists it's true.)

Kristy and I grew up next door to each other on Bradford Court. She has three brothers, Charlie (who's now seventeen), Sam (fifteen), and David Michael (seven). When we were little, I used to envy her big family. Then, soon after David Michael was born, Mr. Thomas abandoned the family. Kristy was so upset. Boy, did we grow close then. And I realized how silly my jealousy had been.

Life was tough for Mrs. Thomas in those years. She found a full-time job and raised the family alone. Kristy tried to help a lot, especially by baby-sitting for David Michael. But one night she couldn't, and neither could her older brothers. Poor Mrs. Thomas called all over Stoneybrook in vain, trying to find a sitter.

What would I have done in a situation like that? Fret, probably. But not Kristy. She calls herself a need-filler, and the description fits. She saw the need: a central number where parents could reach a group of baby-sitters. And she decided to fill it.

The Baby-sitters Club was born, with Kristy as president. It started with just Kristy, Claudia, Stacey, and me. We advertised around town, and before long we were flooded with calls. We began expanding, and we now number ten (including Dawn, who's an honorary member).

Here's how we operate: When a call comes in, we take down the necessary information, then tell the client we'll call back. That's when I go to work. As club secretary, I'm in charge of the official BSC record book. In it, I keep a master calendar that includes all our appointments plus each member's conflicts — doctor and dentist appointments, lessons, after-school activities, and family trips. I can instantly tell who's available, and I try to make sure our jobs are distributed evenly among us.

Some new clients are wary when they learn that we can't guarantee the same sitter repeatedly. They don't look forward to having to train new sitters all the time. But those concerns never last long. Kristy the Need Filler devised a method to keep us all prepared to sit for any client: the BSC notebook. After each job, we write a summary of what happened, making sure to include helpful information about our clients and their kids: new bedtimes and house rules, new hobbies and fears.

Great idea, isn't it? Kristy's full of them. Kid-Kits, for instance. They're boxes filled with old toys, games, and books, which we sometimes take with us to sitting jobs. They don't seem like much, but to kids, they're little treasure chests. You would not believe all the creative events Kristy dreams up for our charges — parties, contests, shows, even a little kids' softball team called Kristy's Krushers.

I miss being Kristy's neighbor. Like me, she moved away from Bradford Court. Nowadays she lives in the wealthy section of Stoneybrook, which is pretty far away. Kristy has to be driven to meetings by her brother, Charlie.

In Kristy's neighborhood, houses like the Kents' are not unusual. No, Mrs. Thomas didn't win the lottery or invent a best-selling video game. She fell madly in love with Watson Brewer, a nice man who just happened to be a gazillionaire. They married, and before Kristy knew it, she was living in a mansion.

You'd be surprised how crowded it seems. For one thing, Kristy and her brothers are all pretty loud, and they tend to take up a lot of space. But Watson also has two children from his first marriage, Karen (who's seven) and Andrew (four), who live there during alternate months. Kristy's mom and Watson wanted a child of their own, so they adopted the most adorable two-year-old girl, Emily Michelle, who was born in Vietnam. To help take care of her, Kristy's grandmother moved in. Add a sweet puppy dog named Shannon, a big old cat named Boo-Boo, two goldfish, a rat, and a hermit crab, and you can picture what life in the Brewer house is like.

Wealth hasn't affected Kristy one bit. She's exactly the same person she's always been. Have you ever heard the saying "The eyes are the window to the soul"? That's definitely true about Kristy. Those brown eyes of hers are always moving, always thinking. But the eyes don't tell the whole story. I think clothes should be included in that saying, too. Kristy's are practical, casual, rugged — just like her.

In fact, clothes say a lot about each of us. If you judge by Claudia's outfits, her soul is crazy and fun and attention-grabbing. (She calls Kristy "wardrobicly-challenged.") To Claudia, putting together outfits is a form of artistic expression, like everything else she does. I have never met anyone as creative as Claud. Painting, sculpting, drawing, jewelry-making — you name it, Claudia can do it well.

You may be wondering why a person so gifted has to repeat seventh grade. Claudia says that her talent in art made the other parts of her brain shrivel up. I don't agree. I think it has more to do with her family. For one thing, Claud's older sister, Janine, is a genius. For another, her parents are very strict and achievement-oriented. The way I see it, Claudia knew she couldn't compete with her sister or live up to her parents' standards. She had to turn to something she could succeed in — art. (I told this to Kristy, and she laughed. She said I should build a stand that says "The Psychiatrist Is In," like Lucy in *Peanuts*.) Anyway, Claudia's schoolwork definitely took a backseat — and I guess it finally caught up with her this year.

Claudia's two other obsessions are junk food

and Nancy Drew novels. She hides them all over her room, because Mr. and Mrs. Kishi allow only healthy foods and "classic literature" in the house. Despite her unique diet, Claudia is not the tiniest bit overweight, and her skin is clear and healthy-looking. She has stunning, jet-black hair and gorgeous almond-shaped eyes. (The Kishis are Japanese-American.)

Claudia, by the way, is our vice-president. She hosts the meetings and answers any calls that come in during off-hours.

Our treasurer is Stacey. She collects dues every Monday. At the end of each month, she uses the money to contribute to Claudia's phone bill and pays Charlie gas money for driving Kristy (and Abby) to meetings.

How would you describe Stacey's soul, judging by her clothes? Sophisticated and worldly. She grew up in the fashion capital of the U.S., New York City, and she dresses in an up-to-the-second, sleek, urban style.

I don't know about you, but I adore the Big Apple. When Stacey talks about growing up near the American Museum of Natural History, riding the subways, visiting galleries and restaurants with her parents, I feel so envious.

Why is Stacey living in Stoneybrook now? Well, she first moved here in seventh grade, when her dad's company transferred him to

Connecticut. She met us and became an original BSC member, and then — *whoosh* — she moved back to NYC because Mr. McGill was transferred again. We thought she'd be gone for good, but the next thing we knew, the McGills' marriage had fallen apart, and Stacey was house-hunting in Stoneybrook again with her mom. (Her dad stayed in the city.) Poor Stacey was devastated by the split-up and all the moving, but we rallied around her. Nowadays she says she has the best of both worlds. Her mom and dad are much happier, and Stacey has a great excuse to visit New York as often as possible.

If you ever come to one of our meetings, you might notice that Stacey is the only BSC member who won't eat sweets. That's because she has a condition called diabetes. Her body can't process sugar properly. If Stacey ate a candy bar, for instance, the sugar would all go right into her bloodstream (in a nondiabetic, the sugar is parceled out a little at a time). This could be dangerous, but Stacey can lead a normal life by staying away from sweets, eating strictly regular meals, and injecting herself daily with a hormone called insulin. (The thought of that makes me queasy, but Stacey says it's no big deal.)

Stacey has long, blonde hair and blue eyes. Until recently, she had a steady boyfriend named Robert Brewster, but they broke up. (One part of Stacey's soul that you wouldn't be able to guess at from her clothing is her broken heart.)

To glimpse Abby Stevenson's soul, you wouldn't have to look at her clothing at all. Just look at her hair. It's wild and curly, and it cascades like a waterfall. That's not a bad description of Abby. She's bubbly and hilarious.

She's also our newest member. The Stevensons moved into a house on Kristy's block not long after Dawn moved to California. The timing was perfect. With one member missing, we were totally swamped.

We almost gained two sitters from the Stevenson family. Abby's twin sister, Anna, turned down an invitation to join. She's a super-serious violinist who practices several hours a day, so she couldn't make the time commitment. (That made me sad. Anna is sweet and quiet and sensitive, and it would have been wonderful to have her in the club.)

Recently Abby and Anna became Bat Mitzvahs together. They participated in a ceremony that thirteen-year-old Jewish girls go through, to celebrate their passage out of childhood and into womanhood. The entire BSC was invited, and the service was so moving, I could barely stop crying.

The Stevenson twins grew up on Long Island, which is in New York. ("Pit-spittin' distance from the Big Apple" is how Abby puts it.) Their mom works for a New York City publishing company. Their dad, sad to say, died in a car accident when the twins were nine. Abby doesn't talk much about him.

Abby is the BSC's alternate officer. She steps in whenever a regular officer is absent. Recently, while Kristy was away on a family trip to Hawaii, Abby filled in as president. Although she wasn't nearly as organized as Kristy, she did a good job. She even put together a fund-raiser for an orphanage in Mexico.

So far, all the club members I've mentioned are thirteen years old. Except for Claudia, they're all in eighth grade. Jessica Ramsey and Mallory Pike are eleven and in sixth grade. They're our junior officers. Their parents don't allow them to baby-sit at night (unless it's for their own siblings), but we keep them busy with jobs during the afternoons.

Jessi and Mallory are best friends. The two things they love to do best are read horse books and complain about how their parents treat them like babies. They're each the oldest in their families. Jessi has an eight-year-old sister named Becca and a baby brother named John Philip (Squirt, for short). Mallory has a huge family — seven siblings, including triplet brothers!

In some ways, Jessi and Mal are quite different. For one thing, Jessi is African-American and Mal is white. Jessi likes to wear her hair pulled back, and she carries herself with super-correct posture. That's because she's a terrific ballerina. She takes lessons in Stamford, which is the city closest to Stoneybrook. Mallory has thick, reddish-brown hair, and she wears braces and glasses. Her main goal in life is to become a writer and illustrator of children's books.

The BSC has two associate members. They aren't required to pay dues or attend meetings, but we turn to them whenever we're overbooked. Logan is one of them. Shannon Kilbourne is the other. She lives in Kristy's and Abby's neighborhood, and goes to a private school called Stoneybrook Day, where she's involved in a million different extracurricular activities.

As I mentioned before, my stepsister Dawn is our honorary member. Whenever she visits Stoneybrook, she comes to meetings. She even takes jobs, if she can fit them in. In California, she belongs to another baby-sitting group called the We ♥ Kids Club.

"He had this accent," Kristy was saying now

about Mr. Kent. "You know, like, 'Quoit rrrroit, thenk you, deah.' "

Abby looked puzzled. "Russian?"

"No, British!" Kristy said.

Rrrrrring!

I reached for the phone. "Hello, Baby-sitters Club," I said. "Mary Anne speaking."

"Yes, K-L-five-three-two-three-one?" a voice said at the other end.

This accent was crystal clear. As British as could be.

"That's right," I replied. "May I help you?"

"Yes, I'm inquiring after a series of fliers I have received regarding what seem to be nanny services?"

"Well, uh, we're not exactly a nanny service . . ." I grabbed a chewing gum wrapper from Claudia's nighttable and scribbled on the back:

It's the Kent mom!!!

I held it up. Everyone fell silent.

"We're just baby-sitters," I said. "You know, middle-school age — "

"Ah. Even better," the woman replied. "The name is Kent. We are seeking a companion for an eight-year-old girl. The child has lived her life in England and is new to the States entirely. She will be attending Stoneybrook Day School. As she is not boarding, her contact with other children will be limited. In the interest of a comfortable acclimation, you see, we thought the child would benefit from an older-sister figure."

The child? What a way to talk about a daughter! I wanted to scold her, but I held it in. Instead, I gently asked, "Well, um, what's her name, Mrs. Kent?"

"I beg your pardon?"

"I asked, what's her — "

"Did you say Mrs. Kent?" The woman chuckled. "Oh, dear, I'm not who you think I am. I'm the nanny."

"Oh!" I could feel myself blushing. "I'm so sorry, Mrs., uh — "

"No need to apologize. My fault entirely for not introducing myself. And it's Rutherford. *Miss* Ursula Rutherford."

"I'm . . . um, Mary Anne!" I squeaked. "Miss, too."

"Mary Anne Mistu," Miss Rutherford said, rolling the *R* and pronouncing the *I* like a double *E*. "Lovely. Sounds like the title of an Egyptian love song. Well, you seem like a reasonable young woman. Could you come for an interview tomorrow?"

I looked around the room. Six pairs of eyes stared back at me in total befuddlement. "Actually, Miss Rutherford," I said, "we do have several qualified sitters, and — "

"Well, I only need one, dear," Miss Rutherford said. "Your address, please?"

My address? I had no idea why she wanted that. "Well, um, one seventy-seven Burnt Hill Road."

"Very good. You will be picked up tomorrow at your house at nine forty-five sharp, if that's convenient."

"I guess — but — "

"Fine. See you then. And do look decent, please. We'll have no sloppy dressing in Victoria's presence. Nor gum chewing, for that matter. She's a delightful child, impish at times, but you know, a princess is a princess, after all."

My throat clammed right up.

"Good-bye," Miss Rutherford barged on. "I look forward to our meeting."

"Buh — " was all I could manage.

As I hung up the phone, I felt numb.

"What did she say?" Claudia asked.

"I — " I swallowed deeply. "I'm going to meet a princess."

CHAPTER 3

My mind was spinning as I left the meeting. I almost walked right past my house.

Now, I do follow world events in the newspaper, sort of, but I had never given much thought to the royal family of England. If you'd told me one of them was coming to Stoneybrook, I would probably have shrugged. I mean, in my opinion, people are people.

So why were my knees shaking as I walked home?

I kept hearing Miss Rutherford's words in my mind: *A princess is a princess.* In less than twenty-four hours, I, Mary Anne Spier the Commoner, was going to be in the presence of royalty. I felt honored. I felt curious.

I felt scared out of my mind.

I pushed open my front door and called out, "I'm ho-o-ome!"

"Hi, home!" answered my father's voice from the top of the stairs.

I hadn't expected him to be there, so early on a Friday. He was on the top-floor landing, dressed in casual clothes and holding a suit on a hanger.

"Dad?" I said. "What are you doing here?"

"Packing," he replied. "I have to go to Wisconsin tomorrow. A huge lawsuit that's blowing up in our faces."

Did I mention my dad is a lawyer? He works for a law firm in Stamford called Harte, Mudge, and Whitman (sometimes known as Hot Fudge and Whipped Cream). He used to work for a smaller firm, but ever since they merged with Hot Fudge, Dad's had to travel a lot.

"Wisconsin?" I said. "How long?"

"Don't sound so sad, sweetheart. I imagine we'll be able to settle in three, four days." He lowered his voice to a whisper. "I'll bring you back a huge pack of top-quality Milwaukee bratwurst. Just don't tell Sharon."

"I heard that!" called my stepmother the vegetarian, from her bedroom. "You will not come near this house with that animal carrion!"

Dad gave me a goony smile. Before he married Sharon, he didn't have much of a sense of humor. Nowadays . . . well, he tries hard. I could tell he wanted to cheer me up.

I smiled back and started up the stairs. "Dad, have you ever known any royalty?"

He thought for a moment. "No, but when I was growing up, I had a dog named Duke. Does that count?"

As I reached the top of the stairs, Sharon barreled out of the bedroom, muttering, "I know I saw it somewhere. . . . I'll find it, I promise."

"My favorite tie's missing," Dad explained. "The maroon paisley one."

"Did you lend it to someone?" I asked.

"No," Dad said.

"Did you leave it somewhere?"

"No."

Sharon was now clattering around the bathroom. Dad and I gave each other a Look.

My dad, I should say, is about as organized as Sharon is absentminded. He color-codes his shirts for daily use, so they wear out evenly. He will not leave one item on his desk when he leaves work. He never misplaces a thing. He still wears a watch he had as a boy.

"The last time I saw it," Sharon called out, "it was all wrinkled. I picked it up and told myself I should take it to the cleaners, but I know I didn't."

As Dad walked into the bedroom to search, I tried to put myself in Sharon's shoes. I closed my eyes and asked myself: If I were Sharon, what would I have done with a tie that was wrinkled?

I thought for a moment or two. I glanced into their bedroom.

Then it hit me. On a hunch, I walked straight to their bookcase and reached between volumes of the Oxford English Dictionary.

I pulled out a folded, flattened paisley tie. "Found it!"

Sharon rushed in. "Where — oh, of course!"

Dad was right behind her. When he saw me, he burst out laughing.

"Well, I just — I have a million things on my mind, and these sudden trips aren't exactly easy to plan for — " Sharon stammered.

Dad smiled and gave her a big, warm hug.

I ducked out. I had enough to worry about on my own.

Somehow I made it through my homework, although I had trouble concentrating. Sharon and Dad were so busy packing that we ordered takeout pizza for dinner.

By the time Claudia came over to do homework, I had managed to put Princess Victoria in the back of my mind. Sitting at the kitchen table, we plunged into our work.

I was giving Claudia a spelling quiz when the phone rang.

I grabbed the receiver. "Hello, Spier residence."

"Guess what? I ate with them."

It was Kristy. She's the only person I know who doesn't feel the need to say hello.

"Ate with who?"

"Whom," Claudia corrected me. (I was impressed.)

"The Kents," Kristy replied. "Watson met the dad this afternoon and invited the family over for dinner. Can you believe it? He was going to cook up a turkey, but he ended up ordering out shrimp scampi. Yecccch. They loved it, though. They thought Watson and Mom had cooked the whole meal."

"What were they like?" I asked.

"Really dressed up. I had to wear a skirt. Mom said the parents were both wearing Georgie O'Mani or something, but it looked like a normal suit and dress to me. The L.P. was wearing this velvet skirt with a ruffly blouse — "

"L.P.?"

"Little Princess. That's what Charlie and Sam and I started calling her — after they left, of course. You know what we had to call the parents? Sir Charles and Lady Kent! Anyway, we all had to keep our elbows off the table, and not reach, and say 'Please' and 'Thank you' about a million times. Then David Michael started picking his nose over his rice, and I thought Mom was going to have a heart attack."

"Maybe *you* should go to the interview tomorrow," I suggested. "I mean, now that you know them . . ."

"No-o-o way!" Kristy shot back. "First of all, the L.P. hardly looked at me. And I felt so stupid I didn't say a word. I hope she likes you better, Mary Anne. She probably will. Gotta go. Good luck. 'Bye!"

"But — "

Click. Too late.

I hung up and swallowed hard. "Kristy met the girl and her family," I said to Claudia. "They don't sound too friendly."

"Uh-oh," Claudia replied.

I stood up and started pacing. "What am I going to do? I'm afraid to go to this interview tomorrow."

"Hey, no big deal, Mary Anne. We just have to plan a strategy, that's all. I can help you with that."

"You can?"

Claudia nodded confidently. "Okay, number one. Most important. What are you going to wear?"

"I hadn't thought about it. A taffeta dress or something?"

"Mary Anne, you're going to an interview, not the royal ball. Wear something simple and elegant, but not too formal."

I thought about that for a moment. "What about a nice pleated wool skirt with a sweater?"

"Perfect. Sort of like a kilt. Conservative, regal, very English."

"Kilts are Scottish."

"Whatever. Then what? I mean, how will you introduce yourself?"

I shrugged. " 'Hi, I'm Mary Anne,' I guess."

"Ugh, Mary Anne, puh-leeze, she's royalty. Maybe something like, 'Greetings, Your Highness.' "

"*Your Highness?*"

"And maybe you should take a few execution lessons."

"*Claud —* "

"You know, like *My Fair Lady?*" With rolled *R*'s, Claudia recited: " 'The rrrrain in Spain falls mainly down the drrrrrain . . .' "

"That's *elocution*. And it's 'on the plain.' "

"What plane?"

"Never mind. I'm just going to speak in my normal voice. And I'll call her Victoria, unless I'm told otherwise."

"Okay. Don't blame me if they banish you to the dungeon."

"Should I know something about England? Do you? Like customs and politics and stuff?"

"Their money is called the pound," Claudia said. "And they drive on the left side of the road. Also, I think the guy who wrote *Romeo and Juliet* was English."

"Shakespeare."

Claudia nodded. "Him, too. And lots of rock groups. Now, the next question is, what will you be expected to do if you get the job? Just baby-sit, or be like a lady-in-waiting — you know, polishing her crown, fetching her soufflés from the kitchen and stuff?"

"She has a nanny, Claudia. I'm just supposed to be a companion, help her feel comfortable in America."

"Easy!" Claudia exclaimed. "You don't have a thing to worry about. Just be yourself."

"Well, that was what I thought I'd do in the first place — "

"And whatever you do," Claudia continued, "just remember, I'll be there with you in spirit."

"Thanks, Claud."

"Feel better now?"

I nodded. "Uh-huh. Um, maybe we should get back to the homework, okay?"

As I picked up the vocabulary page, I pretended I was in a fine mood. Totally back to my normal, happy self. I did not want to tell Claudia the truth.

I was feeling worse by the minute.

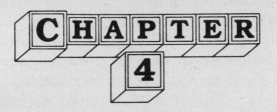

CHAPTER 4

"Richard, your cab is here!" Sharon called from the living room.

My eyes blinked open. I sat up and looked at my clock.

Eight-fifty.

Panic shot through me. In less than an hour, the Kents' chauffeur was going to pick me up. In that time, I had to shower, dress, and eat.

I'd had a horrible night's sleep. I must have turned off my alarm without knowing it.

Dad thumped down the stairs with his luggage. "Wave to the driver," he shouted to Sharon. "Tell him I'll be right there."

First things first. I couldn't let Dad go without saying good-bye. I leaped out of bed and put on slippers and a robe. Tigger, my kitten, slinked into my room and nuzzled my ankles.

"Morning," I said, giving him the world's quickest hug.

I ran downstairs and into the living room.

Sharon was taking Dad's carry-on bag out to the cab. Since I was still in my pj's, Dad gave me a good-bye hug at the door. "I'll miss you, sweetheart," he said.

"Me, too," I replied.

Whoosh. Out to the cab, an embrace with Sharon, and away he went. I waved good-bye from the door and ducked back inside.

I, Mary Anne the Mushy, did not shed a single tear. Yes, I felt a little guilty about that. But my mind was already in overdrive.

The clock in our living room chimed nine. I had to run.

As I ran upstairs, I heard Sharon shout, "I'll make you breakfast!"

Yikes. That was not what I'd had in mind. The last time Sharon had made me breakfast, she'd dropped coffee grinds into the pancake batter.

"You don't need to," I called downstairs. "Really. I can do it."

"Nonsense. I'm not doing a thing right now. You go ahead and get dressed."

I took a deep breath and ran for the shower.

Minutes later I was back in my room, fresh and fragrant, pulling on my plaid skirt and white Oxford shirt.

Beeeeebeeeebeeeebeeee . . .

The sound of the smoke alarm made my heart sink. Not to mention the burning smell.

I could hear Sharon crashing around and saying — well, I won't tell you what she was saying. "Sharon?" I called. "Is everything okay?"

"Fine. Fine. Just a little, uh, toaster trouble. Come down any time. I'll get your coat."

I ignored the smell. I tucked in my shirt, put on a wool cardigan, and pulled on some argyle kneesocks. Then I slipped my feet into penny loafers and rushed back downstairs.

Two empty plates sat on the kitchen table. Sharon was nowhere to be seen, and a crackling sound was coming from the range.

I ran to the stove. A panful of scrambled eggs was turning dark brown before my eyes, with charred, papery edges. On the counter next to it, four slices of pitch-black bread peeked out of the toaster.

I shifted into damage-control mode.

I turned off the burner, switched the pan to a cooler part of the range, and grabbed a spatula. I scraped out what I could, but the eggs were beyond repair.

As I was putting the pan in the sink to soak, Sharon clambered up the basement stairs. "Ohhh, I forgot — "

"No problem," I said.

"I'll clean up," Sharon insisted. "You eat."

I went straight to the cereal cupboard and reached for the Cheerios.

"I don't know where I parked my brain this morning," Sharon said. "I figured your long wool coat would look nice, and I know I stored it in the basement, and — "

"I brought it up here last night, remember?" I said. "Would you like some cereal?"

"Uh, sure, thanks. Gosh, I'm so sorry, Mary Anne."

"It's okay." I took the milk from the fridge and began pouring.

"Apple cider on mine, okay?" Sharon said. "My kinesiologist says I should go off dairy products. I'm not sure why."

I dumped Sharon's cereal and fixed her a new bowl. Then I served us both and started wolfing down my portion. Sharon apologized at least three more times.

I should never have answered her. Or I could have at least waited until I'd swallowed, because during the third "It's okay," a glob of smushed-up Cheerios and milk fell out of my mouth onto my clothes.

Ding-dong!

I jumped straight up at the sound of the doorbell. "My skirt!" I shouted.

Sharon lunged for a sponge. I took it and sopped up the mess as best as I could.

"Does it show?" I asked.

"It's a kilt," Sharon replied. "I think it has Scotch Guard."

40

Ding-dong!

"Coming!" Sharon shouted. Then she turned to me with a warm smile. "You look absolutely wonderful. Don't worry a bit."

We ran to the door. My knees were shaking. I closed my eyes and prepared for the worst.

Sharon pulled the door open.

A man in a gray uniform and cap was standing on our porch. "Morning!" he said with a big smile. "George McArdle. I'm here for the Kents. I believe I'm supposed to pick up Mary Anne?"

An American accent. I don't know why it calmed me down, but it did. I checked my skirt. It looked completely stainless.

I exchanged good-byes with Sharon and followed the chauffeur to his limo. As he held the door open for me, I imagined all my neighbors staring out their windows in awe.

It felt sooooooo cool. I sank back into the soft leather seat of the limo. To my left was a small TV; to my right, a refrigerator.

"Thanks, Mr. McArdle," I said.

"Call me George," he replied as he climbed into the front seat. "You know, I've always loved this house. When I was a kid, I thought it was haunted."

"You live in Stoneybrook?"

He started up the limo and pulled away from the curb. "No, New York. I work for a

Manhattan car service. But I grew up here. Most of our clients work for the United Nations, like the Kents. When I heard they needed a driver to and from Stoneybrook, hey, I jumped at the chance."

We chatted all the way to the Kent house. George was such a nice conversation-maker, I forgot about my nerves.

Well, almost. As we pulled into the driveway, a stout woman with salt-and-pepper hair came out a side entrance of the house and bustled toward us. As George let me out of the limo, she cried out, "Miss Mistu! Welcome. I'm Miss Rutherford."

"Hi," I said, shaking her hand. "Actually, I'm — "

"Come right in. The Kents are eager to meet you."

Miss Rutherford turned and walked back toward the side door. I cast a quick glance back at George and he gave me a thumbs-up.

In I went. Miss Rutherford led me through an enormous kitchen, where a man and a woman were preparing food. "This is Mr. and Mrs. Krull. They're our chefs. Mary Anne Mistu."

"Hi," I said. "Uh, my name is really — "

But Miss Rutherford was already in the next room. "Victoria? Mary Anne is here!"

I followed her through a dining room and

into a big parlor. The first thing I noticed was a large moose head staring at me from the dark wood walls.

The second thing I noticed was a man and woman rising from burgundy leather chairs. The man was handsome and trim, with thinning black hair and a goatee. The woman was tall, with pulled-back reddish-brown hair and blue eyes. She looked as if she could have been a model.

Just beyond them was a roaring fire in a huge, stone fireplace. To its left, across the room from the Kents, a small girl arose from a sofa, where she had been playing with a family of little dolls.

Victoria had dark eyes and silky brown, shoulder-length hair, tied back with a red velvet bow. She was wearing a Laura Ashley floral-patterned jumper, a crisp white blouse, and brand-new suede flats.

I felt as if I were on a movie set. My throat was parched and I hoped they couldn't see the pounding of my heart through my cardigan.

"Sir Charles," Miss Rutherford announced, "this is Miss Mary Anne Mistu."

"So good of you to come," the man said, extending his hand.

My legs locked. I stared at his hand. If Victoria was a princess, what were her parents?

A duke and duchess? Count and countess? Was I supposed to shake his hand or kiss it?

Sir Charles decided for me. He took my hand and shook it. "And this is Lady Kent . . . and Victoria Elizabeth."

After a round of "pleased-to-meet-yous," Victoria sat back on the sofa and picked up one of her dolls. "These are the Wuppertons. They're my doll family."

"Nice," I said.

I lowered myself toward the sofa. Then I thought it might be impolite not to sit nearer to the parents. I froze in mid-squat and cast a glance toward Sir Charles.

"Please," he said with a reassuring nod.

"Dolly Wupperton has a cold," Victoria explained. "I must put her to bed and call the doctor. He's at the orphanage right now because it's flu season."

"Victoria, dear," Lady Kent said, "you'll be excused to the nursery in a moment. But before you become too involved, I'd like to have a word with Miss Mistu."

"Yes, ma'am," Victoria replied.

"It's Spier," I blurted out. "Mary Anne Spier."

Sir Charles cocked his head. "Odd. Miss Rutherford gave us the wrong information."

"Our apologies, Miss Spier," Lady Kent

went on. "Now. Sir Charles and I are each here on special projects for the United Nations. He is a military attaché, and I am in cultural affairs. Although his is a bit briefer project, mine is likely to last six or seven months."

"Both of us will be required to travel abroad quite a bit," Sir Charles went on. "And as prodigiously capable as Miss Rutherford is, she has not been in the States before this. Naturally we're concerned about Victoria's amusement and companionship."

"Naturally," I repeated.

It just shot out of my mouth. I wanted to shrivel up and die. I hoped he didn't think I was imitating him.

"Of course we will meet your organization's customary fee," Lady Kent said. "And your hours will be flexible to accommodate your own schedule."

They both fell silent.

"Uh . . . okay," I said with a shrug. "That's . . . fine with me. I mean, I'll bring it up with the club. You know, at our meeting . . . "

I sounded like a total nincompoop.

"Now, Victoria," Sir Charles spoke up. "Why don't you let Miss Spier accompany you to the nursery."

"Yes, sir." Victoria grabbed her dolls and stood up. "This way, please."

Yes, sir? Yes, ma'am? What a way to talk to parents!

I followed Victoria through the house. She led me to a carpeted, high-ceilinged room with Beatrix Potter wallpaper and a toy cupboard that lined an entire wall. In the middle of the room was a huge Victorian dollhouse. Miss Rutherford was puttering around, straightening up.

"Looks much friendlier since we put up the wallpaper," she said. "Last week it was a hideous gray-brown."

"I liked it," Victoria announced, sitting down next to the dollhouse.

"Well, you'll just have to force yourself to look at Squirrel Nutkin, dear," Miss Rutherford replied with a laugh.

With that, she bustled off.

"Isn't she frightfully *old?*" Victoria said in a loud whisper.

"Well, I hadn't really thought that — "

"Mrs. Wupperton is not quite so old." Victoria knelt by the dollhouse, holding one of the dolls. "She's flying to Brussels tomorrow. So quick, quick — she must kiss Dolly goodbye."

I sat down next to Victoria. "Who's this?" I asked, picking up a primly dressed woman.

"She's Dolly's fat old nanny. Put her down, she has to clean, clean, clean."

I glanced toward the door. Fortunately Miss Rutherford was nowhere in sight.

"Hmmm," I said. "Can I be the doctor?"

"Ohhh, no, he's busy at the laboratory."

"The nurse?"

"You're far too young."

Victoria wouldn't let me be the housekeeper or the older sister or the dog, either. I even suggested becoming an imaginary American friend, named Rachel. To that, Victoria said, "Dolly absolutely can't stand Americans."

Don't worry. When it comes to kids, my ego is pretty strong. I figured Victoria was just letting out her insecure feelings about being in a new country.

"Well," I said, "Rachel feels bad about that. She would love to meet someone from England."

"Of course she would," Victoria said. "Everyone does."

Whew.

I kept trying. I was determined to break through.

It felt like the longest morning of my life. By the time Victoria's parents appeared in the doorway with Miss Rutherford, I had gotten absolutely nowhere.

"Well, how are we getting on?" Lady Kent asked.

"Just lovely," Victoria said dully, without looking up.

"Splendid," replied Sir Charles. "Miss Rutherford, you will work out a visiting schedule, then?"

Miss Rutherford turned to me. "You're available Tuesday, after school?"

"Uh, well, I think so — " I sputtered.

"Very good," Miss Rutherford said.

"Excellent!" Sir Charles echoed.

"Aren't you happy, dear?" Lady Kent asked Victoria.

"Yes, ma'am," Victoria replied.

Me? I couldn't wait to leave.

I think George sensed how I was feeling on the way home. "Don't sweat it," he said. "They're kind of nice when you get to know them."

I sighed and looked out the window. "I felt like I was in the royal court or something."

George laughed. "I wouldn't get my hopes up. The girl is something like forty-seventh in line to the throne."

"Really? I thought she was a princess."

"She is. Technically. They have this whole chain of command. It's called peerage. Has to do with bloodlines. I never did understand it."

When I arrived home, Sharon's car was gone. I let myself in the front door and walked to the kitchen. It was already lunchtime and I was tired, miserable, and starving.

I stopped when I saw an old, scuffed football on the kitchen table.

"Hello?" I called out.

No answer.

There was a note under the football. I rolled the ball aside and read:

MARY ANNE — GONE SHOPPING. HOW ABOUT TOFU — LEEK CASSEROLE WITH GINGER FOR DINNER? YUM!

MOM

P.S. FOUND THIS IN YOUR DAD'S CLOSET. THOUGHT YOU MIGHT BE ABLE TO USE IT.

My mood went from sour to curdled.

Mom? Sharon had never referred to herself as *Mom* before. It made me feel funny.

And what was with the football? Was that some sort of joke? It was so old and disgusting I felt I had to clean off the table.

Not to mention the fact that I hate tofu.

Suddenly the house felt big and empty. I wanted so badly to talk to Dawn. I reached for the phone, until I caught a glimpse of the stove clock. It said 11:58, which meant it was before nine A.M. in California. Knowing

Dawn, she'd be sleeping for at least another hour.

I knew Kristy was in the middle of a sitting job. And who knew where Dad was? Probably still circling around some Midwestern airport.

I slumped into a chair. For the first time all day, tears began rolling down my cheeks.

CHAPTER 5

Sunday

Druscilla is visiting her grandmother Morbidda again. I sat
for her today. Dru, not Mrs.
Porter. Ha ha. Anyway, I
brought my brothers and sister
along and we started the coolest
Thanksgiving project (if I do
say so myself).

Oh, I learned something very
interesting. The English do not
celebrate Thanksgiving at all.
Which makes sense if you think
about it.

Guess how I learned that?

You may have noticed the crossout in Kristy's BSC notebook entry. I think she did that on purpose. "Morbidda Destiny" is the name Karen Brewer gave to Mrs. Porter, their next-door neighbor. Karen is convinced Mrs. Porter is a witch. Why? Appearances, mainly. You see, Mrs. Porter has stringy gray hair, a craggy face, and a wart on her nose. (I'm not being mean. I'm just describing her.)

Druscilla is Mrs. Porter's seven-year-old granddaughter. She has thick, raven-black hair and pale skin. (Karen used to think she was a witch, too, but now they're pretty good friends.) That weekend, Dru's mom had to go on a business trip, so Dru was staying with her grandma.

It was one of those strange, warm November days that can make you think it's summer again. But Kristy wasn't thinking that at all. She had her mind firmly on Thanksgiving.

"The *Mayflower* is about to leave!" Kristy called up the stairs of her house. "All aboard!"

Karen, Andrew, and David Michael clattered downstairs.

"What are we doing?" Andrew asked.

"She already told us," David Michael said as they walked out the front door. "Making a model Pilgrim village."

Andrew burst out giggling. "A pigeon village? That's silly."

"Pilgrim," Karen said. "Those were some of the first European settlers, after the Puritans."

"Doggies!" Andrew shouted.

Karen rolled her eyes. "Settlers, not setters!"

They walked next door, to Dru's. Kristy took a few last-minute instructions from Mrs. Porter. Then, as she left, Kristy laid out her idea: "First we need cardboard, to make a base. Then we cut some plastic soda bottles in half lengthwise and slice off the neck. We cover them with brown paper and grass to make huts — "

"And we can glue dirt to the cardboard for the ground," Druscilla said.

Everyone chipped in with ideas. Within a few minutes, they had a layout for the village, which they named Sodor. (Andrew insisted on that; he's a Thomas the Tank Engine fan.)

Druscilla found a cardboard box in Mrs. Porter's garage. Kristy cut off one side and placed it on the floor of the porch, while the kids ran around looking for materials.

Before long, Linny and Hannie Papadakis, who live across the street from Kristy, had run over to join the hunt. The collection grew to include plastic bottles, tin foil, soil, leaves, and grass.

"Look what I found!" Karen cried, holding up a pigeon feather. "Maybe we can make a headdress."

"Yyyyes! Indians!" Linny cried. "Woo woo woo woo!"

Karen scowled at him. "Native Americans, Linny."

"Yeah!" Hannie agreed.

"Who asked you?" Linny shot back.

That was when Kristy noticed Victoria walking by the house. Miss Rutherford was with her.

"Hi!" Kristy called out.

"Hello," Victoria said. "What are you doing?"

Total silence. The kids' arguments stopped cold. They were staring at Victoria as if she were a visiting Martian.

"Good morning, children," Miss Rutherford called out. "Now, come along, dear. In order to get any exercise, we must keep moving."

"You need the exercise," Victoria said. "I don't. I'm a child. Children don't have swollen ankles."

Miss Rutherford's jaw tightened. Kristy could barely keep from cracking up.

Hannie and Druscilla scampered up to Kristy with excited looks on their faces. "Is that the princess?" Hannie whispered.

"Yes," Karen whispered back. "She had dinner at our house."

"Be polite," Kristy warned them. "Don't ask her any dumb questions."

"We are making a model Pilgrim village for Thanksgiving," Karen informed Victoria.

Victoria looked at them blankly.

"Thanksgiving is an American holiday," Miss Rutherford explained to Victoria.

"The Pilgrims were English people," Kristy said. "I mean, British people. Or whatever. They were being punished for their religious beliefs, so they came here."

Victoria frowned. "Punished? In England? How awful."

"*You* didn't *know* about that?" Linny asked in utter disbelief.

Kristy glared at him.

"That topic is discussed in school when the children are a bit older," Miss Rutherford said.

"We learned it already," Hannie said.

"Heyyy, we know more than a princess!" Linny sang.

"Linnyyyyy," Kristy warned.

"Are you really a princess?" Druscilla asked.

"Well, actually — " Victoria began.

"She is twenty-ninth in line to the throne," Miss Rutherford interrupted.

"You have to stand in line?" Andrew asked.

"No," Linny said. "It's like the president. If he dies, then the vice-president takes over, and if he dies . . . uh, someone else."

"The Speaker of the House," Kristy informed him.

"A speaker?" Andrew looked baffled.

Hannie's jaw was practically scraping the ground. "You mean, one day you could become queen?"

"Yeah, if twenty-eight other people croak first." Linny looked at Miss Rutherford. "Right?"

Miss Rutherford gave him a tiny smile. "Yes."

Everyone started speaking at once:

"If they all catch a disease — " Druscilla began.

"She could challenge them to a duel," David Michael blurted out. "I have this cool sword — "

"If you're a princess," said Hannie, with her hands on her hips, "then where's your crown?"

"You never told us where you lived," Karen added. "A castle, or just a regular mansion?"

"Do you have, like, normal friends?" Linny added.

Andrew pointed at Miss Rutherford. "Is *she* the queen?"

Kristy was cringing. "Guys, don't you have

some collecting to do? Sorry, Victoria. They're just overexcited."

"Perfectly all right," Victoria said. "And I do have friends. Lots of them. In London."

"Want to play with us?" Hannie asked.

Linny elbowed her and whispered, "Say *Your Majesty!*"

"Another time, perhaps," Victoria said.

"Yes," Miss Rutherford said briskly, taking Victoria's hand. "So nice to see you all."

As they walked away, Linny said, "Wow. She even talks like a princess."

"Why didn't she want to play with us?" Andrew asked.

Kristy wanted to scream at them. Instead she turned back to the Pilgrim village. "Come on, guys," she said with a sigh, "before we start another war with England."

CHAPTER 6

"Are you dressed warmly enough?" Sharon asked.

I was at the front door, watching for George and his limo. In my down parka and woolen scarf, I was beginning to sweat like crazy. "I think so."

In two days, the weather had changed from tropical to arctic. (If you live in New England, you know the story.) But I wasn't thinking about the cold at all. I was moments away from The Big Visit. My first official job with Victoria Kent.

"Are you nervous?" Sharon asked.

Nervous? I could barely unlock my jaw. "I'm fine," I squeaked.

With a warm smile, Sharon loosened my scarf and unzipped the top of my jacket. Then she put her hands on my shoulders and said, "Mary Anne, everything's going to be all right. It's just another baby-sitting job."

"Yeah, with the possible future queen of England," I replied.

"Well, that may come in handy someday when you need a place to stay in London."

I laughed. Sharon was being so nice to me these days. I guess she figured if she was going to call herself "Mom," she needed to act like one. (In case you're wondering about the football and the tofu, I handed back one and bravely ate the other. You can guess which was which.)

"Why don't you invite the family over for Thanksgiving?" Sharon asked. "The chauffeur, too. I'd love to get to know them. I'm sure your father would, too."

"Okay, I'll ask."

Light flashed from outside. Looking through the window, I watched George's limo pulling up to the curb.

As I stepped out, I could see our neighbor, Mrs. Prezzioso, taking flash photos from her window. She waved at me with a broad smile.

(Yes, I'm serious.)

Well, George thought that was hilarious. All the way to the Kents', he did a running imitation of a celebrity-TV host: "And no-o-o-ow, for an inside look at the mysterious life of Mary Anne Spier! Our roving reporter has caught her red-handed on a public street . . ."

"George," I said as we drove up the Kents'

driveway, "can you come to my family's Thanksgiving Day party?"

George gave me a big smile in the rearview mirror. "Nice of you. Well, I think I'm working a half-day. I'll ask the Kents and let you know. Thanks, Mary Anne."

Too bad Miss Rutherford wasn't in as good a mood as George was. She met me at the Kents' side door with a curt "Good afternoon. Hang your wrap, please," then immediately turned on her heels and walked through the kitchen.

I draped my coat on a hook just inside the door, then ran to follow her.

"The mater and pater have flown to Europe," she said over her shoulder. "In the meantime, our charge has become a slave to technology."

I had no idea what she was talking about. But I practically had to jog to keep up with her, so I couldn't very well ask.

She brought me into a room I hadn't seen before. In it were a leather sofa, a padded armchair, floor-to-ceiling bookshelves, and a large television set.

Victoria was lying on the floor, watching *Where in the World Is Carmen Sandiego?* In her right hand was a channel selector.

"Doo-doodoo-doooooo!" sang Miss Rutherford, in what I guess was supposed to be a trumpet imitation. "Your companion has arrived!"

"Oh," said Victoria without looking up. "Hello."

Miss Rutherford let out a big sigh. "She's all yours, Miss Spier."

As she bustled away, I sat next to Victoria. "Is it a good show?"

"Too difficult," she said with a frown. Victoria flicked the selector to another channel, which was showing a nature program. "This one is interesting, though. And I adore Bugs Bunny." *Flick.* A cartoon appeared on the screen.

She finally turned toward me, with a look of absolute rapture on her face. "You must watch TV all day!"

"Well, no, not really — " I replied.

"I don't know why. You have so many channels here! In England we only have four. Have you ever heard of anything so boring and backward?"

"Remember, Victoria dear," Miss Rutherford shouted from another room, "our outing!"

"Oh, yes!" Victoria immediately switched off the TV. "On one of your channels I saw an advertisement for the most fascinating place. We *have* to go there!"

For a fleeting moment, I imagined us racing

into the backyard and boarding a small private jet bound for Disney World.

"Everything is there," Victoria continued, "even the largest department store in the world! And I have never eaten at a Friendly restaurant. It sounds awfully good!"

I realized right away what Victoria was describing. "You mean . . . Washington Mall?"

"Miss Rutherford!" Victoria called out. "We're ready! Tell George to bring around the car! Jump to it!"

Miss Rutherford appeared in the doorway, her eyebrows raised high, her fists on her hips. "Yes, Your Majesty. Perhaps I can prepare a flying carpet to take you to the garage?"

With that, she stomped away.

"She thinks she's quite funny," Victoria said, springing up from the floor. "I find her tremendously boring. Come along."

So continued Mary Anne's Day of Following. I followed Victoria to the coatroom and put on my parka again. Through the window I could see Miss Rutherford standing by the side of the limo. She was dressed in a three-quarter-length tweed coat with an enormous crocheted scarf around her neck.

Victoria grabbed a beautiful, butter-soft suede jacket from a hook.

"It's very cold outside," I said.

Victoria shrugged. "The mall is indoors."

"Victoria, please, put this on." I took a down coat off another hook.

Victoria stared at me blankly. Then she whirled around and banged on the glass of the door. "Miss Rutherford, my companion is tormenting me!"

Tormenting? I couldn't believe my ears. "All I said was — " I began.

Miss Rutherford opened the door a bit. "Did she tell you to put on a thicker coat?"

"Yes!"

"Then *you're* tormenting *her*. Hurry up, the petrol won't last forever in the tank!"

With a sigh, Victoria switched coats and walked outside. Under her breath she muttered something that included the words "absolutely horrid."

Which, to be honest, was a perfect description of my mood just then.

I decided something that afternoon. I hate limos.

People would not stop staring at us as we drove to the mall. At a red light, a guy in the car next to us rolled down his window and yelled, "Yo, who's in there?"

George answered, "The President of the United States!" then sped off when the light turned green.

It wasn't the last nosy question. By the time

we pulled into the parking lot, we had been the Byzantine Emperor and his entourage, the Ambassadors to Neptune, and Whitney Houston's band.

I was happy to walk into the mall with Victoria and Miss Rutherford in their normal-looking coats.

Victoria squealed as we entered the main rotunda. "Ohhhh, it's *exquisite!*"

I almost cracked up. I mean, I guess it is pretty nice, as malls go, but I'd never seen that kind of reaction before.

"It's one of the largest in the country," I told her.

"Is that why they named it Washington?" Victoria asked. "After George Washington, the father of your country?"

Miss Rutherford gave a hiccupy kind of hoot that must have been a laugh. "Our little historian."

By the central fountain, Victoria spun around, looking upward to the five glass-rimmed balconies overhead. "Oh, we *must* go into every single store!" she said.

"Providing at least one is a foot-care emporium," Miss Rutherford grumbled. "I *am* human, after all."

Well, we didn't go into every store, but we wandered for about an hour. We watched a life-sized Santa being propped up in a card shop window. We bought a bag of caramel corn to snack on. Victoria announced she was "disappointed" with Macy's, because it didn't seem like the world's largest store. (I explained that its flagship store in New York City was the one that made the claim.)

Have you ever shopped with an eight-year-old who has a credit card? I don't recommend it. Victoria felt she could have anything she wanted. If it weren't for Miss Rutherford, she would have bought a projection TV with four speakers, an electric kid-sized car, and a Rottweiler. As it was, she did buy a Barbie set, a kids' CD player, a collection of Tom Chapin and Bill Harley CDs (on my recommendation), a huge bag of exotic-flavored jelly beans, a couple of helium-filled Mylar balloons, a dress at Steven E, and several T-shirts to send home to her friends.

Or, rather, I should say she ordered the items for delivery. Miss Rutherford refused to carry them out.

After a haircut and about a half hour in front of a video machine, Victoria demanded a snack.

"Hallelujah," Miss Rutherford muttered wearily.

I was exhausted, too. Honestly, I thought

shopping with Stacey McGill was difficult, but this was in a class by itself. A nice, quiet snack at Friendly's would be perfect.

But when Victoria saw the noisy, crowded, fast-food burger place, she screamed, "Oh, we must eat here!"

"*Oh, now, really*, Victoria," Miss Rutherford humphed, "we'll be in line for hours."

"I don't care," Victoria replied.

"The food isn't that great," I tried.

"Oh, yes, it's very special! We have one of these in London, and the lines are always much longer. Come!"

She grabbed my hand and dragged me toward the glass doors.

Well, the line was long. The food was dreary. But I must admit, seeing Miss Rutherford's face when she bit into a chicken nugget was almost worth the trip.

"What on earth is this made of?" she asked.

"Chicken," said Victoria, who was making quick work of a double cheeseburger.

"Processed gristle, no doubt," Miss Rutherford remarked, gobbling another in one gulp. "Although it doesn't taste bad, if one ignores the texture."

Victoria and I washed down our meals with milk shakes (Miss Rutherford had tea, which she found "revolting"). As Victoria opened a small pack of cookies, she asked, "Have you ever been to New York City, Miss Spier?"

"Mary Anne," I corrected her. "Sure I have."

"Is it as abfab as the mall?"

"Oh, much more so. Especially at this time of year. Everything is all lit up. There's a Christmas tree as tall as a building, music everywhere — "

"Then you simply must show me around there! We can visit my parents at the United Nations when they return."

"Return?"

"Yes. They've been in Brussels since Saturday."

"Ohhh, that's too bad," I said. "My father's on a business trip, too. I know how you must feel."

Victoria shrugged. "You know, they're always flitting around — flit, flit — but they'll be back."

I was amazed at how casual she seemed. Deep inside, she must have been missing them. I sure was missing Dad.

"Oh, I almost forgot!" I exclaimed. "How would you like to join us for Thanksgiving dinner?"

Victoria said nothing. Miss Rutherford wiped her lips with a handkerchief and replied, "I believe Sir Charles and Lady Kent will be away that week as well."

"That's even more reason for you to come over," I said. "Both of you. So you won't feel lonely."

Miss Rutherford gave me a hint of a smile. "When we return to the house, I shall check the schedule."

Well, the schedule (or SHED-yool, as Miss Rutherford pronounced it) turned out to be clear. I found that out two days later, on my next visit to the Kents'. Miss Rutherford accepted my invitation, on the condition that Victoria did her homework before I left.

We went right to work. Victoria had to answer questions about the book *Stone Fox*, by John Reynolds Gardiner, which her class had been reading. (*Stone Fox* was one of my favorites as a child; I cry just thinking about it.)

I figured Victoria would hate the book. It takes place in a rural American town, and it's about a boy who enters a dogsled race to win money that will prevent the bank from taking over the farm where he lives with his dying grandfather.

Not exactly a regal kind of story.

But I learned something about Victoria. She identified with the boy completely. She was so smart and sensitive. I could even see the trace of moisture in her eyes as she talked about the ending of the book.

I felt I was finally breaking through. And that gave me hope.

Victoria came along on the drive home, but she insisted we stop at Pizza Express for a quick slice. (I didn't mind at all, because Sharon had promised steamed kale with onions and garlic for dinner.)

My third visit with Victoria was after the football game that Saturday. (SMS had won, by the way, which meant the team was going to be in the championships the next week.) When Miss Rutherford led me into the nursery, Victoria was waiting with a tape recorder and mike.

"This is Mary Anne, saying, 'pair of ears,' " she said, thrusting a microphone toward me.

"What — why — " I stammered.

"Go on!" Victoria urged me.

"Pair of ears," I said softly.

Victoria turned off the machine. "Pairrrrr of earrrrs. Hmmm. Now say the word, 'schedule.' "

"Victoria, why are you doing this?"

"To study. I adore the way you speak, Mary Anne. You know, it reeeeeally isn't harrrrd to sound like an Amurrrrican."

I couldn't help laughing. "You *want* to sound like an American? But your accent is so beautiful."

"Hardly. All the children at school seem

to find it silly. They giggle so, every time I speak."

My heart went out to her. No child likes to feel picked on, not even royalty. "That's just because they don't know you well," I said. "Maybe we can invite some of them over."

Victoria shrugged. "Perhaps. I haven't really made friends with any of them yet. They don't talk much to me. And I'm not fond of them, either. They're not at all like my friends in London, Jezra and Annabelle and Christina. I have spoken to Druscilla, though, in the corridors. She's awfully mature, for a second-grader." She cocked her head. "You don't say ma-TOOR, do you? I heard someone say ma-CHUR, which sounds a bit like a sneeze — "

"I have an idea," I said. "Next week is the big football game for Stoneybrook Middle School — "

"I play football in my school in England!" Victoria exclaimed.

"Great, then you'll know more about the game than I do. Anyway, my boyfriend is on the team, and I was planning to go with a bunch of my friends. We can invite Druscilla and Karen and some other kids your age."

All the excitement in her eyes faded. She shrugged and looked away. "I suppose. You'll have to check with Miss Rutherford, of course.

And if I do go, I may bring along my cassette recorder."

"Sure, Victoria, whatever you like."

"You know, Mary Anne, you really are a splendid companion," Victoria said with a tiny smile. "Now. Read aloud from *Stone Fox* into the microphone, but be sure to speak slowly . . ."

I did as she asked (or *commanded*). But while I read, my mind was spinning.

A splendid companion. Had Princess Victoria actually called me that? I could hardly believe it. What did I do to change her mind?

Maybe nothing. Maybe this was the way she acted with all the people she liked.

Or maybe she was just loosening up. Finally saying what was on her mind.

Just what was on Victoria's mind? It was so hard to tell. Did she hate Americans or admire them? Was she really cold-hearted about her parents, or was she trying to cover up a hurt deep inside? Was she too shy for friendships, or too snobby?

The football game was a good idea, I knew it. But it was only a start.

I had to bring Victoria out. It was my job to make her happy.

Well, not just a job. I wanted to help her.

I was actually beginning to like the little princess.

CHAPTER 7

"Hi, sweetheart!"

Two words were enough. I could recognize from the tone of my dad's voice over the phone that he did not have good news.

"Hi," I replied. "Are you coming home tomorrow?"

Dad took a deep breath. "Well, I'm afraid that's what I was calling about. It seems the plaintiff blah blah deposition rutabaga litigator peas and carrots change of venue . . ."

No, that wasn't exactly what he said. The precise words didn't matter much to me. But their meaning did: Dad was going to be delayed.

This was the third time. He'd called six days earlier to say he'd be spending the weekend away. Then he'd called Monday to say he needed until Thursday.

Now Thursday was here, a week before

Thanksgiving, and Dad was still in Milwaukee.

"Anyway, I do have good news," Dad continued. "The judge put his foot down today and said he refuses to let the case go beyond next Wednesday, so that we can all go home to our families and have something for which to be thankful."

"So you'll be gone until Thanksgiving Day?" I asked.

"I'm afraid so."

I guess that was good news. I suppose the case could have dragged on until Christmas.

I tried to sound upbeat. We talked awhile longer, then I gave the receiver to Sharon. She didn't seem any happier about the news than I was.

As Sharon hung up, she heaved a big sigh. "Well, we can either sit here and moan over your father, or cheer ourselves up."

I smiled. "I vote for the second."

"Good. Let's go shopping at the mall. I need to buy some Thanksgiving trimmings and order a turkey and all that — "

"A turkey?" I asked. I was expecting some disgusting vegetarian substitute.

Sharon shrugged. "Sure. You and your dad will eat it. And we need to teach your princess and her governess about American traditions, don't we? Besides, I'm going to cook up some yams and a rice dish you won't believe, all of which will make me happy. Now . . . after we order the bird and do all that boring stuff, maybe we can pick a nice, new winter sweater for you?"

"Seriously?"

Sharon grabbed her car keys off the kitchen table. "Let's go."

I was so excited. I really did need a new sweater. As we ran outside, I scolded myself for all the negative thoughts I'd ever had about Sharon.

It felt kind of nice to drive to Washington Mall in a normal car, although I did miss the glamour a bit. (I missed the smoothness, too. Sharon is not exactly easy on the brakes.)

At the mall, our first stop was a gourmet shop. "May I help you?" a smiling clerk asked.

"I'd like to reserve a turkey," Sharon told him.

"Smoked, glazed, or Native American traditional seasoning?"

"Just regular," Sharon replied. "You know, raw."

The guy looked as if Sharon had just ordered fried walrus. "Uh, this is a gourmet shop? We specialize in prepared foods?"

"Oh." Sharon looked embarrassed. "Of course."

Prepared. That was a key word. It meant *no cooking for Sharon*. As positive as I was trying to be, I couldn't shake a mental image of Miss Rutherford discovering a bracelet in her stuffing.

"You mean, all we'd have to do is heat it up?" I asked.

The clerk nodded. "I've got quite a few smoked birds, frozen and ready to go. I recommend them. We've had tons of happy customers."

We agreed we'd pick one up on the way out.

Whew.

Next stop, Macy's, where we bought beautiful cloth napkins and candles. On our way out, we passed the most gorgeous display in the designer clothing section.

In the center of it was a cotton sweater, thickly woven and bursting with fall colors. It reminded me of a sweater Dawn had bought during her first experience with New England cold weather.

"This is nice," Sharon said, fingering the material. "It really says *you*."

If my dad had been there, I knew just what he'd do. He'd nod solemnly, look at the price, then mutter about finding a cheaper "department-store knockoff."

"Well, I'm sure there's a cheaper one like it — " I began.

Sharon burst out laughing. "You sound like your father. Look, he's there and we're here. If he can buy bratwurst, I can buy this for you."

I didn't quite follow the logic, but I didn't pursue it. Before I could close my gaping jaw, Sharon had found a sales clerk and plunked down her credit card.

My feet were barely touching the ground as we left the store. I must have thanked Sharon a hundred times.

After about her ninety-seventh "You're welcome," Sharon stopped in front of a store called *About Face*. "Oh, isn't this stuff cute?"

The window was crammed full of crazy accessories — barrettes, headbands, hats, and buttons. Now, I happen to love *About Face*. Awhile ago, I received a terrific free makeover there. But I wasn't wild about most of the stuff on display. And my stomach was growling with hunger.

"That headband on the left would look nice, wouldn't it?" Sharon said.

I looked where she was pointing. It was a broad band with a light-blue, psychedelic summery pattern. It was beautiful, but frankly, I'm not really a headband kind of person.

"You mean, for you or for me?" I asked.

But Sharon was already inside, flagging down a saleswoman. I waited near the door, admiring my sweater.

A moment later, the saleswoman was handing me the headband, so I put it on.

The woman looked at me skeptically. "To be honest, I see this on someone with longer hair and lighter coloring."

"Oh, well," Sharon said. "Never mind."

Good. Lunchtime.

As we headed toward the escalator, a woman ran up to us. "Sharon!"

Sharon smiled broadly. "Hi, Regina! Mary Anne, Regina is someone I volunteer with at Meals on Wheels. She lives in Mercer. Regina, this is my daughter, Mary Anne."

Stepdaughter. The word almost flew out of my mouth. I had to fight back the urge. How could I even feel such ingratitude, after what Sharon had done for me?

"Hi," I said.

Regina left us at the next floor, and Sharon and I went on to the food court.

At the sight of the Friendly's sign, my stomach felt like a dog with a wagging tail. "Mmm," I said, "I could go for a nice, juicy — "

"Cracked-wheat-and-cabbage crock pot!" Sharon said.

At first I thought she was joking. Then I saw that she was reading from the blackboard menu in front of the Bountiful Wellness Macrobiotic Restaurant. "Perfect!" she went on. "We loved that last time we were here, remember?"

The truth? I had never set foot in that restaurant in my life. And I doubt I ever would have loved anything with cracked wheat and cabbage in it.

The day's events suddenly became clearer to me. The Dawn-like sweater . . . the Dawn-like headband . . . the Dawn-like meal . . .

Okay, Sharon had been generous and warm to me that day. I was grateful for that. But I had to wonder. Exactly which daughter was she seeing while she did all these nice things? Was it really me? Me, Mary Anne Spier?

Or was I a stand-in for Dawn?

As we walked into the restaurant I had a sinking feeling. Like an actor who's suddenly found herself onstage in the wrong play.

CHAPTER 8

"O y heahboy declay-or that ye Froiday meeting of thou Baby-sittuhs Club shall come to or-dah!" said Kristy.

Claudia's room fell silent.

"Were you just at the dentist, Kristy?" Jessi asked. "You sound like you have a mouth full of Novocain."

"Ha ha," retorted Kristy. "That was my royal British accent, if you please."

"Ugh, Shakespeare is rolling in his grave," Claudia said with a groan. "He is dead, right?"

"I think you mean *English* accent," I said to Kristy.

"What's the difference?" Kristy asked.

I was ready with that answer. Victoria had informed me. "Well, *English* means from England. *British* could mean anywhere in Great Britain. For example, something relating to Wales would be considered British."

"Like blubber?" Claudia asked.

Now it was Mallory's turn to groan. "Wales, not whales."

"Ahem," said Kristy. "Any new business?"

"Yes," I said. "I want to bring up Victoria. I've met with her four times now, and — "

"You're ready to jump out a window," Abby continued.

"No, I wasn't going to say that," I said.

"You're too polite," Kristy remarked.

"I like her," I insisted.

"Every time you talk about her," Stacey said, "you're always saying how closed-off she is."

"That's true," I agreed, "but it's not her fault. The poor girl is only eight, and she's in a new country, a new house, a new school — and her parents aren't even around to help her adjust. Imagine how you'd feel."

Abby rubbed her chin, as if in deep thought. "With a limo and a credit card at my disposal, and a house the size of an airplane hangar? Hmm, give me a minute to think about this."

"All I'm trying to say," I went on, "is that deep inside, Victoria is just a little girl who's having trouble fitting into a new environment."

"Not enough red carpets here in Stoneybrook, huh?" Stacey asked.

"Look, I know what you're thinking. She's snobby. She expects people to obey her every

80

command. She doesn't seem to care what people think of her. But you have to understand, she grew up in a different world than we did. With different rules. In England, she's in the so-called ruling class. People are expected to act a certain way. Here in the U.S., where everyone's lumped together, she doesn't know how to act. So what do the kids in her school do? They ignore her. Maybe they're afraid of her. And at home, she's kept practically under lock and key by her nanny. She has no real friends."

"Shannon told me that her sister, Maria, asked Victoria to come over to her house," Kristy reported. "Victoria refused."

"Maybe she felt shy," I said. "Look, our phone number was probably one of the first numbers the Kents called when they moved here. When I accepted the job, I did it on behalf of the BSC. So as I see it, we're in this together. We should all seriously try to help Victoria out. Make her feel welcome."

Claudia nodded. "Any suggestions?"

"Well, I've already invited her to the football game tomorrow," I began.

"Easy enough," Abby said. "I'll come along. I may need a ride, though — I mean, if there's enough room in the limo . . ."

"You'll have to squeeze in with me and Karen," Kristy said.

Jessi laughed. "Wait until I tell Becca. She's dying to meet Victoria. All week long she's been talking in this princess voice she made up. It's very cute."

"I can ask Charlotte Johanssen to come with me," Stacey suggested. "She's the same age as Victoria."

"This is great!" I said. (Neither Charlotte nor Becca had met Victoria, because they go to Stoneybrook Elementary School, not Stoneybrook Day.) "Victoria's already excited about going. She told me she plays football in England — "

"A princess playing *football?*" Mallory said.

"Pahdon me, would you pleeease pahss the pigskin?" said Kristy in a terrible accent, as if she were asking someone to pass the tea.

"Kristy, don't be offensive," Stacey said.

"That's like asking a bird not to fly," Claudia muttered.

"I heard that!" Kristy sprang out of her chair and began whapping Claudia with her visor.

Rrrrrringg!

A phone call brought the meeting back to order again.

I grabbed the receiver. "Hello, Baby-sitters Club, Mary Anne speaking."

"Hey, Mary Anne, this is George, the driver. Miss Rutherford told me I'd find you here."

"Hi, George!"

"I'm calling to say I talked to the Kents, and they said it was okay for me to come to your party with Miss Rutherford. So I accept!"

"Great!" I replied.

What good news. Things were really falling in place. Thanksgiving was going to be great fun, and our plan for Victoria was about to begin.

When I arrived home, I found a note attached to the refrigerator by a magnet:

HI, M.A.!
   COULDN'T FIND ANY BREAD
IN THE HOUSE. BE BACK
SOON. MAY ALSO RENT
A VIDEO. THE PETER, PAUL,
AND MARY CONCERT MIGHT
BE INTERESTING.
               X XX O O O,
                  MOM

I thought for a moment. I checked the bathroom and the living room. I finally discovered a loaf of seven-grain bread behind a throw pillow in the den.

Oh, well. Maybe we could eat extra sandwiches while we were watching Peter, Paul, and Mary.

As I made myself a toast-and-honey snack, the phone rang.

My heart clenched. I just knew it was Dad. Telling us he'd be gone until the new year. Or that he'd be transferring my school records to Milwaukee.

I picked up the receiver. "Hello, Spier residence."

"Hi, Ms. Residence, it's your sister."

"*DAAAAWWN!*" I screamed. I couldn't help it. "Boy, am I happy to hear your voice. How are you?"

"It's eighty-seven degrees out, we were released early from school because of teacher conferences, and I'm calling from a cell phone from the poolside at Maggie Blume's house. That's how I am."

"Beam me over, Scotty!" I said.

We cracked up. Then we both started yakking at once. She filled me in about her latest adventures with the We ♥ Kids Club. I told her all about Victoria and my plan to make her feel welcome.

Dawn stopped me when I mentioned Thanksgiving. "You mean, you invited her to your house?"

"Yes," I said, "plus her nanny and chauffeur."

"And you're serving the traditional brutally massacred, decapitated, and scorched bird carcass?"

"Uh, yeah." (Dawn, as you can see, has

84

strong views about meat-eating, although *occasionally* she eats non-red meat — but apparently not Thanksgiving turkeys.) "But your mom is making some non-meat dishes."

"Good. I hope she doubles the ingredients."

"Well, I'm sure she expects some of us to — wait, what are you saying? You're not — "

"I am."

"You — you are?"

"Yup."

"*Coming here? For Thanksgiving?*" I was screaming again.

"Dad already bought me the ticket! Oh, Mary Anne, I miss you and Mom so much. Dad said I could do this, as long as I promised to spend Christmas with him."

"That's great! I mean, not that you're not coming for Christmas, but that your dad said — oh, you know what I mean! When are you coming in?"

"Thanksgiving morning. I'm taking the red eye, so I won't be there until five after nine in the morning."

"Great. We'll all pick you up."

"No!" Dawn shot back. "Mary Anne, I want this to be a surprise to Mom. Maybe Richard can sneak out by himself and pick me up."

"He's in Milwaukee on business, but he's coming back that day."

"Well, maybe we can come home together in a cab."

"Great."

"But whatever you do, no spoiling the secret, okay? Except for BSC members. Maybe they can come over!"

"Can I write Dad and tell him?"

"Well, I guess, because we'll meet at the airport — but swear him to secrecy, too!"

"Okay!"

Dawn let out a loud giggle. "I can't wait! 'Bye!"

" 'Bye!"

When I hung up, I was flying. I didn't care what kind of video Sharon brought back. I could watch a tape of a golf tournament or a broccoli quiche bakeoff.

My sister and my dad were coming home for Thanksgiving. That was all that mattered.

Well, almost. It would be nice if SMS won the championship football game. Might as well have a happy Logan at the party, too.

CHAPTER 9

Saturday—

I know—I'm only supposed to write about sitting jobs. Well, today I'm not. But this is important information for anyone who intends to sit for my little sister. You will need to know some new things about her.

For one thing, she wishes everyone to know she is no longer Becca Ramsey. She is now Crown Princess Rebeccazzar of Greater Ramseyland...

"**M**y subjects, I am ready for my toasted waffle!" commanded Becca Ramsey as she swept into the kitchen, a plastic tiara on her head and a cotton blanket wrapped regally around her shoulders.

The edge of the blanket clipped Jessi's bowl of Rice Krispies, dragging it toward the edge of the table. "Hey!" Jessi shouted.

"Waffo!" squeaked Squirt, her baby brother. He banged on the tray of his high chair, toppling over his plastic milk bottle.

Jessi dived for her bowl. The bottle clattered to the floor.

Jessi's aunt Cecelia turned from the kitchen counter, where she was buttering toast. "I don't believe I heard a 'please' anywhere in that question."

Princess Rebeccazzar sat calmly at the head of the table. "Fetch my waffle or I shall summon the Lord High Executioner!"

"Did someone call me?" Mr. Ramsey thumped downstairs, still dressed in his robe and pajamas.

"Off with Lady Cecelia's head!" Becca cried.

Mr. Ramsey recoiled in horror. "But it might fall in the toast!"

Jessi's dad is pretty funny. He also has a beautiful, deep voice. Jessi keeps telling him he should quit his job and become an actor.

(He laughs at the idea, but he has done two voiceovers for the advertising company Mrs. Ramsey works for.)

Aunt Cecelia is Mr. Ramsey's sister. She does not have a beautiful voice. Nor much of a sense of humor. According to Jessi, she can be a pain. She lives with the family and helps take care of Squirt.

"Everybody eat up," said Mrs. Ramsey as she walked into the kitchen. "The fuller you are, the warmer you'll be at that football game."

Squirt held out his bottle. "Baba!"

"The Prince Regent would like his royal milk," Becca informed everyone.

"Prince Regent?" Jessi said. "What does that mean?"

Becca thought about that a moment. "I don't know . . . prince of the whole regent?"

The Lord High Executioner laughed. So did Lady Cecelia. That made the Prince Regent clap hands and spill a bowl of rice cereal.

Princess Rebeccazzar suffered the indignity of having to get her own waffles.

Becca is eight years old. She's actually a pretty shy girl, but she has a rich imagination. On the day Becca heard about Victoria, her little princess routine began.

Now that Becca was about to meet Victoria, the routine was going overboard.

Jessi and Becca wolfed down breakfast, then ran off to get dressed and washed up. They left the house at 10:10. Arm in arm, they hurried down Kimball Street toward the school.

"I cahn't wait to meet my royal frrrriend," Rebeccazzar said.

"Becca, she'll like you just the way you are," Jessi reassured her.

"What if she doesn't?" Becca asked.

Jessi shrugged. "It'll be her loss."

They arrived at the field the same time Claudia and I did, around 10:20. (The game was to begin at 11:00.) "Hi!" I called out.

"Greetings, my subjects!" Becca said.

We all met up with Stacey, who was with Charlotte Johanssen near the refreshment stands. Charlotte was bundled up in a thick woolen coat, her red hair tucked into a beret. Stacey looked very . . . well, *Stacey*. She was wearing a black baseball cap, black sunglasses, and a sleek, black, ankle-length coat with sharply padded shoulders.

Mallory arrived next, with her ten-year-old triplet brothers, Adam, Byron, and Jordan. "Where's the princess?" asked Adam.

"Here I am!" replied Rebeccazzar of Ramseyland. "No flash photos, please."

"Boring," Adam replied.

Jessi took Becca aside. "Now, when Victoria arrives, promise me you'll be yourself again."

"Jess*iiiii* — "

"I mean it, Becca. She'll think you're making fun of her if you play Rebeccazzar."

"I *know!*"

At that moment, the limo pulled up to the curb. Everyone — I mean *everyone* — turned to look. The few people already in the bleachers were peeking through the slats.

The rear door opened. Kristy stepped out first, waving to the crowd like a celebrity (what a ham). Next came David Michael, then Karen, Druscilla, Abby, and Victoria.

George had agreed to take the whole neighborhood to the game.

Last out was Miss Rutherford. She did not look as if she'd had a happy ride.

"Heyyyyy, everybody!" Kristy said. "Victoria, come meet my best friends."

She introduced everyone. Behind her, Miss Rutherford was looking around, wary and uncomfortable, as if she'd just wandered into the Stoneybrook Zoo by mistake. Victoria calmly smiled, shook hands, and said things like "Pleased to meet you," and "Charmed."

"Doesn't she talk cool?" David Michael said with a proud grin, as if he'd taught her the accent himself.

"What does 'chommed' mean?" Becca whispered to Jessi.

"*C-H-A-R-M-E-D,*" Jessi spelled out.

"Testing . . . testing one . . . two . . ." a voice blared over the P.A. system.

"Let's go, before the good seats are taken!" Kristy sprinted into the stands, signaling us to follow.

Of course, practically no one was there yet. We sat near the fifty-yard line, halfway up the bleachers.

It was gray and chilly. Miss Rutherford was clutching her scarf as I helped her up the bleacher steps. She wiped a spot with a handkerchief, then sat. "Are we permitted to leave after the first team scores?"

"Uh, no. Here's how it works . . . " As I patiently tried to describe the game to Miss Rutherford, Kristy chipped in with the finer points of downs and penalties and strategies.

Out of the corner of my eye, I caught a glimpse of Logan. He was sprinting along the track around the field with a group of teammates. When he spotted me, he gave a little wave. One of the other guys, Clarence King, saw this and made a kissy face. (So mature.)

As for Jessi, she was busy eavesdropping on her little sister. Becca was in the middle of an entourage around Victoria — including Druscilla, Charlotte, David Michael, Karen, Adam, Jordan, and Byron.

"Well, in *our* public school in England, we board," Victoria was saying.

"We're pretty bored in ours, too," Byron said solemnly.

"Don't you go to a private school there?" Charlotte asked.

"Oh, yes," Victoria informed her. "We call private schools *public* schools, though."

"You have it backward," Adam said flatly.

"Where do you boys go to school?" Victoria asked.

"Stoneybrook Smellementary," Jordan spoke up.

"P.U.!" Byron cried out.

"It's free," David Michael said.

"Free?" Victoria looked baffled. "Are you wards of the state, like Oliver Twist?"

"Oh, *dear*, not *we!*" slipped the voice of Princess Rebeccazzar from the mouth of Jessi's sister.

"Beccaaaa!" Jessi warned her, then quickly added, "Our parents pay taxes, and that covers the schools."

"Well, then, they *are* paying!" Victoria said. "So you *do* go to a public school. There. You see?"

The kids fell silent at that.

I quickly changed the subject. "Victoria says she played football in England."

"Who-o-oa!" Byron's eyes were wide. "A football-playing princess?"

"Pretty cool, Your *Hike*-ness!" Adam blurted

out. "Get it? Because in football, when you say, 'Hike' — "

"My favorite position is goalie," Victoria barrelled on.

"*Goalie?*" Jordan burst out laughing. "Uh, *wro-o-ong*, Vickerooni!"

I thought Mallory was going to throttle him.

But Victoria didn't seem to notice the insult. She was looking out onto the field. "Those boys have awfully broad shoulders. Their uniforms make them look like robots. And who on earth has the ball?"

"You can't see the ball?" Adam repeated. "Maybe you can borrow my sister's glasses."

"Their ball is the brown oblong thing, dear," Miss Rutherford explained. "You see, Americans are very literal. They devised a football that resembles an actual foot."

"But I see them *throwing* it," Victoria remarked. "In football, you must kick it, unless you're the goalie — "

"You're thinking of soccer," Karen said.

"Europeans call soccer football," Abby explained.

"Really?" Byron asked.

"Cool," Druscilla said.

"Chomming," added David Michael.

"Well, then, if the players are permitted to throw the ball, it should be called a *hand*-ball, and that's all there is to it!" Victoria announced. "Now, I'm awfully hungry. I thought I saw bangers when we came in. Please fetch some for me, would you, Miss Rutherford?"

"Bangers?" Charlotte said. "What are they?"

"Bang! Bang! Bang!" David Michael pretended to smash the triplets over the head with a sledgehammer.

"You call them hot dogs," Miss Rutherford said. "And I refuse to suffer the slings and arrows of outrageous indigestion — "

"I simply *adore* bonkers!" Rebeccazzar piped up.

"You are what you eat," Jordan murmured.

The triplets started whooping and giving each other high-fives. (Rebeccazzar was not pleased.)

"I'll start a food run," Claudia volunteered.

"Yeeeaaaa!" The kids all stampeded to the concession stands with Claudia. I closed my eyes and hoped that Victoria would begin making friends while in line.

They returned a few moments later, armed with cardboard trays full of hot dogs, cotton candy, nuts, and soda.

Victoria made quick work of two hot dogs, pronouncing them "exquisite."

Becca sat next to Victoria. As the game started, Becca tried to explain all the rules (which basically meant asking Kristy and repeating Kristy's answers).

Whenever Victoria convinced one of us to go back down to the concessions (which was often), Becca tagged along. Whatever Victoria bought — which included food, a couple of Stoneybrook pennants, a bumper sticker that said I ♥ SMS, a bullhorn, a noisemaker, and an SMS cap — Becca would carry back.

At one point, I leaned over to Jessi and whispered, "They're becoming best buddies."

"Maybe . . . " Jessi looked skeptical.

Together we watched. Becca wasn't the only one trying to gain Victoria's attention. Charlotte tried to start modest little conversations about school. Karen told a couple of funny stories. The triplets made dumb jokes.

Victoria was slowly warming up. She was smiling shyly and trying to answer everyone's questions.

At halftime, I heard David Michael ask, "Isn't football great, Vic?"

That was when Victoria lit up. "Vic! You know, that is a wonderful nickname. It's so American. Not boring old Vic . . . toe . . . ree . . . ahhh. Mary Anne, will you promise to call me only Vic when we're in New York City?"

"Are you going to New York City?" Stacey asked. "I grew up there."

"Splendid — I mean, grrrreat! You can be our guide."

"Whoa, wait a minute," I said. "When is this trip?"

"Wednesday," Victoria said.

"Victoria discussed this with the mater and pater this morning," Miss Rutherford spoke up. "She has neglected to inform you that her parents returned to the States last night."

"Oh, I'm sure they read the papers," Victoria said. "Anyway, we'll have room for one more, too, my mother told me."

"Me! Me!" screamed Charlotte, David Michael, Druscilla, Karen, and the triplets.

"Not a child, though," Victoria replied. "Kristy, *you* come. There, it's settled. Mary Anne, Stacey, Kristy. And Miss Rutherford, if her feet permit her. What a fabulous time!"

Victoria let out a cheer and rattled a noise-maker.

"I want to go home," David Michael said glumly.

"Me too," grumbled Druscilla.

I could see Victoria's friendships floating away like an out-of-bounds football.

How was the game? Well, Stoneybrook won. And Logan scored a touchdown, which was so fantastic. I was proud of him. The crowd went absolutely crazy, too.

97

I think David Michael had a good time. And Karen had brought along a book, which seemed to absorb her during the second half.

Druscilla didn't say much during the game. She seemed distracted. Charlotte complained of being too cold, so Stacey left early with her. The triplets had decided to stay as far away as possible from Victoria, and Mallory spent most of the game trying to force them to behave.

Miss Rutherford, of course, complained politely about the seats, the weather, and the complicated rules of the game.

Because Stoneybrook had won the championship, we left the stands surrounded by screaming, dancing fans.

Some of that spirit rubbed off. But mostly, the kids were itching to go home.

Jessi said her sister seemed down and out when they arrived home. So she managed to convince her mom and dad to take the family out to an early dinner.

You know how kids are. Becca's dreams of a sleepover at Buckingham Palace had been dashed, but she cheered up just fine.

From that day on, though, Princess Rebeccazzar was never again seen in the Ramsey house.

CHAPTER 10

"Absolutely not!" Kristy said, folding her arms.

The second order of business in our Monday meeting had been whether Kristy, Stacey, and I could go to New York City on Wednesday. (The first order had been telling everyone about Dawn's visit and organizing a late Thanksgiving Day get-together. Everyone had said yes.)

Convincing Kristy about this one, however, was not going to be easy.

"Kristy, be reasonable," Stacey pleaded. "We have a half day Wednesday. George has said he'll pick us up from school at noon. We'll have practically the whole day in New York City" (this was something of an exaggeration) "during the holiday season! It's a once-in-a-lifetime opportunity."

"Can he drive us home in time for the meeting?" Kristy asked.

Claudia rolled her eyes. "Kristy, lighten up. It's the day before a family holiday. Parents aren't going to be calling for sitters. The rest of us will be here. We'll run a Meeting Lite."

"The skeleton crew," Abby said, "that's us."

"Look," Kristy retorted, "we just finished our probation. If we all just skip out of a meeting for any old excuse — "

"It's not just some silly excuse, Kristy," Mallory said. "Three of you have been invited to the United Nations by English royalty."

"Besides, Victoria is one of our charges," I said. "Think of this as a job."

"We might cause an international incident if we refuse," Stacey said.

"Who knows? You might end up on TV or something," Claudia said.

"Great publicity for the BSC," I added.

Kristy nodded her head slowly, as if deep in thought.

Stacey and I gave each other a Look. An *I-can't-believe-she's-even-thinking-about-this* look. I crossed my fingers.

"Okay," Kristy said. "But the rest of you have to show up five-thirty *sharp*. I'll be checking in by phone. And Mary Anne and Stacey, we have to be camera-ready — BSC T-shirts on at all times!"

The idea of wearing our T-shirts over our parkas was ridiculous. Stacey knew it and I knew it. But we were both so totally delirious with happiness, neither of us said a word.

That night, after my homework, I found Sharon in the den, leafing through a family album.

"Hi," I said softly.

"Oh, hi, Mary Anne." Sharon's voice was a bit husky. "Want to sit down?"

I did. I glanced at the album. The pages were yellowing, and some of the photos were falling out.

Sharon tucked in a shot of Dawn as a newborn, perched precariously on her lap. "She was always doing that, you know — practically falling out. She wanted so badly to walk." She turned to a photo of her and Mr. Schafer, holding Dawn at about age three on a surfboard. "Look! Look at that one. The surfer who owned this board was majoring in Irish folklore. He used to tell Dawn stories about a white horse from the mystical land of Tir Na n'Og under the sea. Dawn wanted to surf out and pay a visit."

Tir Na n'Og? How on earth did she remember stuff like that?

"Oh, and here's the first time we took Dawn to Disneyland . . ."

As Sharon went on and on, I smiled and listened. I could tell how much she missed Dawn. I didn't blame her. I missed Dawn, too.

Part of me was just dying to tell her the secret, to blurt out that Dawn was coming home for Thanksgiving. Maybe then Sharon wouldn't feel so sad.

Maybe then she'd relax and enjoy the daughter she had right there with her.

I don't remember much of Tuesday, and Wednesday morning was an excited blur. After school, George was standing outside by the limo. A crowd of about ten kids had gathered around him.

"Hi!" I called out, as Kristy, Stacey, and I approached.

"Hello," George replied. "I was meeting some of your good friends."

The rear door flew open and Alan Gray, the Dork King of the Eighth Grade, leered out. "Grrrrreetings! Will you shoo them all away, Jeeves, and take me to the bank so I can climb a pile of my own money?"

Kristy stormed up to the open door. "If you're not out of there by the count of five, Alan, I will personally climb in, sit on your lap, and kiss you."

Kristy didn't even reach 1. Alan was sprinting down the street, screaming "EWWWWW!" at the top of his lungs.

"Would you really have done that?" George asked.

Kristy grimaced. "Do I look stupid?"

We all climbed in. George drove us straight to the Kents'.

Victoria was practically bursting with excitement as she climbed in the backseat. In her right hand she was holding a small flash camera, and she began snapping away.

Miss Rutherford settled herself with a lot of huffing and grunting. "Now," she announced, "there will be no eating or reading in a moving vehicle, or I will have Mr. McArdle immediately turn around and come back."

George turned around and peeked through the limo's divider. "I could use the ejector seat," he said. "You're sitting on it, Ursula."

"Oh!" As Miss Rutherford jumped out of her seat, George pulled away from the curb.

"Fasten your seatbelt, please," Victoria scolded her.

The five of us sat facing each other on the two bench seats. As we rolled out of the neighborhood and toward the expressway, I was all tingly.

"I have never been to New York in such style!" Stacey said.

"Let's do some funky things," Victoria piped up.

Miss Rutherford gasped. "Young lady, please!"

"What? Doesn't that mean 'fun'?" Victoria asked.

"Well, not exactly," Kristy said.

"Oh, do teach me American slang," Victoria pleaded.

"How about American songs?" Stacey said. "Those are fun for car rides."

We sang songs that never end, like "Jon Johnson" and "Michael Finegan." We sang "If I Had a Hammer," and "This Land Is Your Land," and the coolest song called "Turn the World Around."

When we reached "Follow the Drinking Gourd," Victoria directed us to "correct" her pronunciation of *gourd*, with a hard *r*.

"Gourd," Stacey said as we sped down the Connecticut turnpike.

"Gourrrrrrrd," Victoria repeated.

Stacey giggled. "Now just ease up . . . *gourd*."

Victoria's eyes grew focussed and intense. "Lord," she said.

"Uh, yeah, same idea," Stacey said. "Just put a *g* — "

"No, I mean, lord, look at those buildings!" Victoria cried out.

Stacey turned. George had just passed a thick grove of trees, and the New York City skyline stood in front of us, beckoning.

"'A holiday bite of the Big Apple,'" read Kristy from a brochure Miss Rutherford had picked up somewhere, "'has a touch of cinnamon and cloves, a cool tartness that keeps you on your feet, yet a sweetness and warmth that reminds you of home.' Yechh, who writes this stuff?"

"Sounds marvelous to me!" Victoria said, her nose pressed to the car window. "I mean, *cool*. Sounds way cool to me. Ooooh, this is so lovely. Can we climb out and walk?"

"Across the Triboro Bridge? I don't think so," replied Stacey.

"Where are we going first?" I asked.

"To a powder room," Miss Rutherford said. "Preferably in a large, comfortably appointed department store."

"Great, Saks Fifth Avenue," Stacey replied. "That'll put us right in the middle of all the good holiday stuff. We're not meeting your parents until five, so we should have time to see the windows, the tree at Rockefeller Center, and FAO Schwarz."

"Oh, wayest cool! We're meeting a friend?" Victoria asked.

"That's a toy store."

"Is it near the U.N.? I'm sure my parents will want to join us and take us to the loveliest restaurant — "

"May I take this opportunity," Miss Rutherford interrupted, as the limo swung onto the F.D.R. Drive on the East Side of Manhattan, "to review the rules of inner-city travel. At no time are we to lose sight of each other or the car. At all times, Victoria must be holding hands with one of us, preferably two of us. We are to avoid eye contact with suspicious individuals, crossing to the other side of the street if necessary."

"Oh, bother," Victoria said. "How can we tell how *bad* they are if we don't make eye contact? Personally, I intend to leap up and kiss anyone like that."

"Impudence is not a desirable quality in a city like New York, where young children are lost at the rate of . . . well, many a day! Now gloves are recommended, as the amount of surface grime creates an unhealthy breeding ground for microbes . . ."

Miss Rutherford droned on about pickpockets and subways and dirt. Each time she gazed out the window, Victoria would cross her eyes or make a face. Kristy, Stacey, and I could barely keep from cracking up.

George steered off the highway and onto the streets. Immediately we were in bumper-to-bumper traffic. Horns blared around us, and pedestrians wound their ways between the cars, clutching shopping bags.

"It looks rather like London," Victoria said. "Oh, you three simply must come to London! Will you?"

"Sure," Kristy said. "Maybe George can drive us."

"You bet!" George called out. "I'll use my jet car."

"Oh, I wish you had one now," Victoria said. "I want to go straight to Bloomingdale's!"

"We're right around the corner," Stacey remarked.

"Pull over right now!" Victoria shouted.

"Absolutely not!" Miss Rutherford said. "To Saks Fifth Avenue, as planned, Mr. McArdle. We shall enjoy the sights from our comfortable seats and be grateful."

We passed under the big Roosevelt Island tram. We drove past the crowded sidewalks of Bloomingdale's. We waved to people in a long line at Radio City Music Hall. At one point, we even caught the tiniest glimpse of Central Park.

As we inched past a horse and carriage on Fifth Avenue, Miss Rutherford said, "Simply dreadful, that those beasts should be subjected to this treatment!"

"That's what the horses are thinking about us, cooped up in this smelly car!" Victoria said.

I had to admit, I agreed. Seeing New York from the back of a limo in heavy traffic was dull. We might as well have been watching a video.

"There's Saks!" Stacey said, pointing ahead.

"Very good," Miss Rutherford said. "I shall go and freshen up. Mr. McArdle will find a parking space, while you wait for me."

Before Victoria could scream bloody murder, George made a sound like a game-show buzzer. "*Ehhhhhh*. False. Parking is not allowed on these streets. I'll have to drop you off. Look, you're supposed to meet the Kents at five. How about I meet you in front of the Plaza Hotel at four forty-five? Right near the golden statue of the horse and rider. Anybody know where that is?"

"Sure!" Stacey said.

"Oh, dear . . ." Miss Rutherford murmured.

"We'll take care of Victoria," Stacey said.

"Yyyess!" Victoria cried out, a little awkwardly.

109

"And we'll stand guard for you outside the bathroom door," Kristy added.

As we left the car, Miss Rutherford's face was as red as the holiday decorations.

Well, it took us awhile to reach the ladies' room. The first-floor aisles were full of store employees spraying free perfume samples, and Victoria insisted on sniffing every one.

After Miss Rutherford's pitstop, we wandered through the store, trying on hats and scarves and sweaters — generally having fun while Miss Rutherford skulked around watching for serial killers or something.

Even though it was not yet Thanksgiving, the dark wood-paneled walls were draped with pine boughs and twinkling lights. With holiday spirit in the air, and the knowledge that my dad and sister were going to return the next morning, I felt just wonderful.

Not to mention the fact that Victoria seemed to be having the time of her life.

After Saks, Stacey led us across the street, toward Rockefeller Center. On the corner of Fiftieth Street and Fifth Avenue, several food vendors stood side by side. The sweet aroma of hot, honey-coated peanuts competed with the smoky smell of roasting chestnuts.

I thought I was going to drool right on the sidewalk.

"I *must* have some of those chestnuts!" Victoria demanded.

We walked down the block toward Rockefeller Center, stuffing our faces and giggling like crazy.

"Look up," Stacey said all of a sudden.

I did. First I saw an army of trumpeting angels, sculpted out of thick white wire and arranged in two lines down a gentle hill. Beyond them was a skating rink. And beyond that, framed by the angels' upraised trumpets, was the Rockefeller Center tree.

How was it? Spectacular, even though it wasn't yet lit. It was seven stories high (I counted), and surrounded by people snapping photos.

Kristy was the first to notice that Victoria was gone. "Vic?" she called out.

"Oh, dear." Miss Rutherford began to shake. "Oh, my word!"

"*VIC!*" Kristy bellowed.

"Yes?" a bewildered-looking businessman answered.

We left him there and bolted down the slope, screaming Victoria's name.

Stacey, Kristy, and I found her leaning over the railing, watching the skaters.

"I thought I spotted David Letterman," she squealed, "doing a pirouette!"

"Victoria, don't ever do that to us again," Stacey scolded.

As we lectured her about sticking together, Miss Rutherford stormed toward us, huffing and puffing. "Victoria, I have half a mind to tie your wrist to mine!"

"You do so and I shall become a Pilgrim," Victoria said defiantly, "and move to the United States to escape you."

"Look," Stacey said, "we'll walk together up Fifth Avenue. If any of us is separated, we can meet at our checkpoint in front of the statue at Fifty-eighth Street. George will be there waiting."

We all agreed. Victoria, however, wasn't concerned at all about being lost. She took photos of the tree. She took photos of us, surrounding a chestnut vendor. As we walked up Fifth Avenue, she kept shouting, "Get yer chess-nuts heah — eat 'em while they're hot!"

We visited a camera store and a bookstore. We bought chocolates at Godiva (Stacey settled for a soft pretzel from another vendor). We wandered into St. Patrick's Cathedral.

Finally we reached the Plaza. It's a pretty glamorous-looking place, with flags lining the front and people climbing in and out of limos. Just across the street from it are the low stone walls of Central Park.

"Hey, let's skip the hotel and check out the park!" Kristy said. "We have time."

"Over my dead body!" Miss Rutherford said.

"It's the coolest place!" Stacey said.

"Way coolest," Victoria agreed.

"I will agree to take you girls for tea at the Plaza," Miss Rutherford said. "But that is as far as we shall go."

"Oh . . . gross," Victoria said.

Actually, tea at the Plaza didn't sound bad to me at all. We trudged up the stairs and inside the main corridor.

Victoria gasped. "This was where the boy in *Home Alone 2* stayed, wasn't it? I saw that in London, you know."

Miss Rutherford was admiring the windows of the shops that line the Plaza's lobby. "Lovely," she said.

As she wandered around to the left, melting into the crowd, Victoria shot away to the right.

Kristy went after Victoria, and I turned to call for Miss Rutherford. But Stacey grabbed my wrist hard. "Ssshh," she whispered. "*She's* the one wandering away. We're not supposed to look after her."

"Stacey!" I said. "We can't just let her go. That's not right!"

"Look, you're supposed to be a companion

to Victoria, not Miss Rutherford. Besides, we said we'd meet at the statue if we separate, right? And we have to be there in a little while, anyway." With a big grin, Stacey pulled me in the direction Kristy had gone. "In the meantime, let's have some fun!"

CHAPTER 12

Wednesday

FOR THE EYES OF BSC MEMBERS ONLY!!!
MAY NOT BE USED IN A COURT OF LAW

When the NYC police come to get me,
tell them I did it for the sake of the
monarchy. Or something like that.
But seriously, folks, I just couldn't
bear another minute with Miss
Rutherford. I mean, I know my
hometown. I'm NOT worried or
intimidated in the most crowded
place on earth at the most crowded
time of the year! So what was
the harm in taking our own little
mini-tour of the Big Apple?...

Until I read that, I hadn't realized how guilty Stacey had felt about leaving Miss Rutherford.

She sure didn't seem that way as she explained to Kristy and Victoria what we'd done. Victoria's reaction?

"Waaaay cool!" (Of course.)

"The Central Park Zoo's open until five," Stacey went on. "Want to go?"

"A zoo!" Victoria shouted. "Gross! No, that means bad. I mean, cool — oh, I have them mixed up. Yes, let's go!"

I looked over my shoulder. Miss Rutherford was nowhere to be seen. I had to run to catch up with Stacey, who was leading Kristy and Victoria out a side door of the Plaza.

At the corner, we crossed the street and walked into Central Park. It was crowded with families, and we wound our way through them.

"It's a small zoo," Stacey said. "But it's great."

She's right. I've been to that zoo a few times, and I never grow tired of it. I loved the tropical house, which felt like an indoor jungle in the middle of Manhattan. I enjoyed watching monkeys scamper around outdoors. Victoria loved the sea lions, but she was most fascinated by a polar bear who kept swimming the same pattern back and forth across a small pond.

"Poor thing," Stacey said. "I read in the newspaper that he's seeing an animal psychologist."

I thought that was pretty hilarious. I imagined the bear stretched out on a couch.

Victoria wanted to go into the penguin house but Stacey had other plans. "To Schwarz!" she announced.

FAO Schwarz is right across the street from Central Park. Victoria enjoyed that even more than the zoo. Especially when a life-sized toy-soldier model turned out to be a real person who burst out into song!

We were upstairs, watching an enormous electric train set, when Stacey cried out, "Yikes! It's four-forty! Time to go."

"Ohhhh, can't we just *live* here?" Victoria asked.

"Bring it up with Miss Rutherford," Kristy said.

We raced out the door. The tour had been short, but a lot of fun.

As we approached the statue, though, my heart was in my mouth. What we'd done was kind of stupid. Miss Rutherford would probably be frantic. What if she'd had a heart attack worrying? What if she'd called the police, or Victoria's parents?

George was standing outside his limo, right near the statue. "Heyyyy!" he called out. "You guys are right on time. Where's Miss Rutherford, taking a jog around the park?"

Stacey's eyes were focussed on the front doors of the Plaza. "I don't think so . . ."

Miss Rutherford was bustling down the steps, flanked by two policemen and a dark-suited man holding a walkie-talkie.

"Oh, dear," Victoria murmured.

"Yo! Miss Rutherford!" Kristy cried out.

Miss Rutherford stopped in her tracks, then started talking a mile a minute to the men.

Then they began walking toward us. I could see the words *Plaza Security* stitched onto the dark-suited man's jacket. "Everything all right?" he asked.

"Yup," said George. "Thank you for finding Miss Rutherford."

Miss Rutherford gasped. "Finding *me*? Why — of all the — how — ?"

"Are these the children, ma'am?" one of the police officers asked.

"Yes, they are," Miss Rutherford replied. "And thank you."

As the men left, Miss Rutherford shot me a Look. I thought she was going to explode. "Miss Spier, if you ever — "

"It was my idea, Miss Rutherford," Stacey spoke up.

"We had such an awful time!" Victoria exclaimed. "I mean, *awesome!*"

"Well," Mrs. Rutherford replied, through gritted teeth, "we have much to discuss with the Kents. Let us go."

She didn't say one word on our trip to the United Nations.

George dropped us off in front of the building. Once inside, we were treated as if we were international spies. We had to go through metal detectors, sign papers, and answer questions before we could even reach the elevators. Kristy told one official that she was an ambassador from Stoneybrook, but he didn't find that very funny.

Sir Charles and Lady Kent had offices in the same area of the building, but neither was in. At 5:02, we sat down in the waiting room of Lady Kent's office.

At 5:27, we were still there.

Finally, Lady Kent burst in from the hallway. "Hello, darlings. Oh, you're all *so* patient. Your father will be here presently, Victoria. Do come in."

She led us into her inner office.

"Uh, Lady Kent," Kristy said, "would you mind if I made a call to Stoneybrook from your phone?"

"Go right ahead," Lady Kent replied.

As Kristy went off to make her check-up call

to the BSC, Miss Rutherford cleared her throat. "Lady Kent, I do feel it my duty to inform you that — "

"Oh, Mother," Victoria said, "we have had the most radical time. We've seen the *coolest* animals at the zoo, and the tree — wow!"

"Ahem," Miss Rutherford interruped her, "as I was saying — "

"Hello-o-o-o, children!" Sir Charles said, strolling in, "how was our little excursion today?"

"Just the way grossest!" Victoria exclaimed.

"Coolest," Stacey whispered.

Sir Charles's face stiffened. "I'm not sure I understand."

"Oh, Father, it was, like, so amazing! I have never seen such a large Christmas tree. And the shops are grrrreat!"

"Do your pretzel-guy imitation, Vic," Kristy called out, her palm over the receiver.

"Vic?" Lady Kent said.

"Get yer re-e-e-ed hot chess-nuts heah!" Victoria shouted.

Sir Charles's smile had frozen. "My, I see we've picked up quite a bit of the . . . street argot, haven't we?"

"Oh, and we saw so many restaurants!" Victoria barreled on. "When we drive back I'll show them to you. I wouldn't mind which one you took us to!"

Sir Charles and Lady Kent exchanged an uncomfortable glance. "Ah, I'm not sure why you had the impression we were joining you for supper, dear," Sir Charles said.

Victoria's smile vanished. "You're not?"

"Well, much as we'd love to, it's quite impossible," Lady Kent added. "Your father and I will be in meetings, in preparation for our trip. As you know, we leave straight from the office tonight."

"Which is why we were so eager to see you here, now," Sir Charles said.

"Oh," replied Victoria.

"Well, everything's fine!" Kristy cheerfully announced, as she sat down on the carpet.

No one replied.

"Did I say something wrong?" she asked. "Uh, I can pay you for the call."

"That won't be necessary," Lady Kent said.

She and Sir Charles kept asking Victoria questions, but boy, had Victoria's mood changed. Her answers were mostly yeses and nos. Miss Rutherford did manage to mention that we'd all been separated at the Plaza, but the Kents seemed more angry at her than at Victoria.

When it was time to leave, Sir Charles said, "Eat at the finest restaurant you've seen, Victoria. French, Italian — whatever cuisine you choose! Now, come give us a kiss."

We said our good-byes and left. Victoria was completely silent as we walked to the elevator.

Stacey, Kristy, and I exchanged a Look. None of us knew exactly what to say.

"Well, that was awfully nice of your father, wasn't it?" Miss Rutherford finally said. "A nice French meal would be quite lovely, I think. After a day like today we could stand something quiet, civilized, elegant."

"Where would you like to go, Victoria?" asked Stacey.

The elevator door opened and we all stepped in. "I believe I saw a Pizza Hut on the way here," Victoria said. "I won't go anywhere else."

Zhoop. The door slid shut. You should have seen the look on Miss Rutherford's face. (Stacey's, too.) I don't think Pizza Hut was what they'd had in mind.

"Sounds good to me," Kristy chimed in.

"What's street argot?" Victoria asked.

"Slang," Miss Rutherford said. "I don't think your parents approve."

Let me tell you, after that tense scene, it was great to see good old George. He drove us to the Pizza Hut and waited at the curb. (We ended up taking him a few slices with onions.) Since the Kents weren't coming, Stacey called to invite her dad.

You know what? He showed up ten minutes later in a cab! He actually paid for the meal, even though Victoria had her parents' credit card.

Afterward, Mr. McGill rode with us to the American Museum of Natural History. The streets to the north and south of the museum were closed to traffic. There, we watched preparations for the Macy's Thanksgiving Day Parade.

What a scene. If you think those balloons look huge on TV, floating over the crowd, you should see them spread out on the streets. Each one is the size of a house. They're held in place with heavy netting. It takes a team of workers to tend each one. The helium is pumped in from enormous tanks, and the balloons rise, section by section.

Stacey's dad bought us hot chocolate and tea from a nearby deli. As we sipped, all huddled together, we watched the Cat in the Hat lift slowly upward.

In the windows of the apartment building across the street, we could see families gathered together, looking down on the festivities. In the amber light of their living rooms, they all looked so warm and cozy. Just above the Cat in the Hat's head, we caught sight of a little girl in pj's, standing with her mom and dad and waving to us.

We waved back, until the cat's hat blocked our view of them.

I looked down at Victoria. She was wiping her face with her coatsleeve. Her eyes were very red.

Stacey had noticed, too. "Are you okay?" she asked.

Victoria said, "Let's go home now."

CHAPTER 13

Victoria was asleep when George pulled up to the curb in front of my house. Her head was nestled in Miss Rutherford's lap.

"So, let me get this straight," George whispered over his shoulder. "I'll pick you up here tomorrow morning at eight, and we're meeting a nine o'clock flight at the airport."

"Yes," I whispered back. "Actually, we're meeting two flights. My stepsister will be on one of them, but my stepmom doesn't know about that. I told her that Miss Rutherford volunteered your services, but just to pick up Dad."

"Why would Ursula do something generous like that?" George asked with a wink.

"Ahem," Miss Rutherford said.

"I said it was out of gratitude for being invited for Thanksgiving — and for my last couple of weeks with Victoria." I gave Miss

Rutherford a glance. "I guess that's stretching it, after what happened today."

"You do strain my capacity for forgiveness," Miss Rutherford said with a sigh. "But on the whole, I must admit I can't imagine what I'd have done without you."

Whoa. That was the nicest thing she'd ever said to me. "Well, good night. It was fun."

" 'Night," whispered George, Miss Rutherford, Stacey, and Kristy.

I blew Victoria a kiss. Sleeping, she looked much happier than when she'd been awake. I felt so awful for her.

As I stepped out, Kristy gave me the high sign. "Good plan, too. For the airport pickup. Couldn't have done it better myself."

Pulling out a bag of souvenirs I'd bought, I shut the door gently behind me.

I checked my watch as I walked up my front lawn. Eleven fifty-one.

Yikes. I hadn't realized it was that late. I hoped Sharon wasn't too worried.

I let myself quietly in the front door. Sharon's voice floated in from the kitchen. "I think that's her now," she was saying.

"Hi!" I called out.

"Mary Anne?" Sharon shouted. "Come on in. Your father's on the phone."

I rushed in and set down my souvenir collection — a small Macy's balloon, a Planet

Hollywood T-shirt, some Godiva chocolates, and about twenty postcards.

On the kitchen table I noticed a family photo album, open to pictures of Sharon's and Dad's wedding.

Still in my down coat, I took the phone from Sharon. "Hi, Dad! Oh, I can't wait to see you! I'll be picking up you and — I mean, you, *in a limo!*"

(Ugh. I almost said, *you and Dawn.*)

"Very spiffy," Dad replied. Then he dropped his voice to a whisper. "You didn't tell Sharon the secret yet, did you?"

"No. Uh, on our way home, I'll tell you all about my trip to New York, okay?"

"Great. I'll tell you all about the hotel conference room in Milwaukee. So you should have plenty of time."

I laughed. "Great. See you at the airport."

"You bet," Dad replied. "I'll be the fellow with the ear-to-ear grin. Love you, Mary Anne."

"Love you, too."

As I hung up, Sharon said, "Excited, huh?"

"Yup!" (I didn't tell her the *whole* reason, of course.)

"Your dad is, too. You know what he told me? In a funny way, he likes long trips, because they remind him of how much he loves his family."

"That's so . . . corny," I said with a giggle.

But you know who I was thinking about? Victoria. I wondered if her parents felt the way my dad did. I wondered if they had ear-to-ear grins when they returned from trips.

"So," Sharon said, "you're home awfully late. You must have had a good time."

"I guess," I said, taking off my coat. "But Victoria thought her parents were going to join us for dinner. You should have seen her face when they said they weren't. And the worst part is, they're flying overseas tonight, straight from New York."

Sharon shook her head. "No wonder the poor kid is the way she is."

"What do you mean?"

"You know, so standoffish. So unable to make friends. She's afraid of being close to anyone."

"I don't get it, Sharon. I mean, if she's so lonely wouldn't she *want* to make friends?"

"Sure. But put yourself in her shoes. What happens to all the people in her life, all the ones she loves?"

"Well, her parents fly away all the time," I replied. "But she probably has friends and family in England."

"Yes." Sharon nodded. "And she's here. How would you feel about all that if you were an eight-year-old?"

I thought a moment. When I was around eight, I grew very curious about my mom's death. I had fears that everyone close to me was going to die. It was only a phase, but boy, was it painful. "You think she's afraid she'll always lose her loved ones? It's kind of hard to imagine that strong little girl being scared."

"She's strong for a reason." Sharon looked absently down at the photo album. "It's funny, but I know how she feels. I guess I'm an expert on losing family members." She winced. "Ugh, I didn't mean for it to come out that way. It's just that, after it happens to you enough times, you blame yourself. As if you drove them away or something. If you don't watch it, you start to be afraid of loving anyone. You think maybe *that* person will leave, too. And your heart will be broken all over again."

I knew Sharon was talking about Victoria. But I had another feeling, too. "Do you feel that way about Dawn and Jeff?"

Sharon's smile wavered. Her eyes grew moist. "Well, yes, I suppose. But I hope I haven't seemed cold and standoffish to you, Mary Anne."

"No!" I protested. "Just the opposite!"

"Yeah, I guess I've been kind of a nuisance lately." Sharon laughed. "We all react differently to loss, Mary Anne. I suppose I tend to wallow in it. Looking at photo albums, trying to live in the past . . ."

I thought of the trip to the mall. I thought of all the ways that Sharon tried to fit me into Dawn's mold.

I still wasn't happy about it. I still wished she'd see me as me. But I wasn't mad about it anymore.

When Sharon spoke again, her voice was low and subdued. "You know what, Mary Anne? If you were gone I'd do the same thing."

"You would?"

Sharon nodded. "That's the way I am with the people I love. I can't help it."

Hoo, boy. Forget it. My eyes just flooded up. I gave Sharon a great big hug.

The photo album slid off the kitchen table. It fell open to a page of photos from the wedding reception, with Dawn and me clowning around for the camera.

Sharon and I sat there, rocking slowly over the images, until our eyes were dry.

CHAPTER 14

"Wait," Sharon said. "Wait. If I want the turkey to be ready by noon, shouldn't I put it in right now?"

I swallowed my last spoonful of Crispix cereal and wiped my mouth. "It's pre-cooked, remember? All it needs is warming up."

"Oh. Right."

"Are you sure you don't mind me leaving?"

I had to ask it. I just had to. But if she said yes, I'd probably scream.

It was Thanksgiving morning, and I was about to be picked up for my trip to the airport. I was a wreck. My stomach was a tightly wound knot. I hadn't realized how hard keeping a secret could be. Staying home was the last thing I wanted to do.

"Nahh," Sharon said. "I know how much your dad is looking forward to seeing you. I can handle the rice and yams and health loaf."

"*Health loaf?*" I exclaimed. "Why are you making that?"

Health loaf is Dawn's favorite — some all-veggie kind of meatloaf substitute. Had Sharon figured out the secret? Had I said something by accident? Blurted it out in my sleep?

"Because it happens to be the one dish I make the best," Sharon said with a laugh. "And I love it. Even if you don't."

I smiled. I nodded sweetly. I was not going to give away a thing.

I just hoped I wouldn't barf up my Crispix from nervousness.

The limo arrived as I was clearing the table. " 'Bye!" I shouted, grabbing my coat and running outside.

" 'Bye!" Sharon answered.

George greeted me with a loud "Good morning," and opened up the rear door of the limo.

Inside, Victoria was sitting all alone, watching a cartoon on the TV. I hadn't known she'd be coming, but I was happy to see her.

"Hi, Vic," I said.

She glared at me, then looked back at the TV. "Victoria, if you please."

"Sorry."

As the limo rolled away from the house,

George said, "We're not in the best mood today."

"Is everything all right?" I asked.

"Fine," Victoria said. "I could not *wait* to leave the house. Miss Rutherford is preparing herself for the party. Being with her would have been frightfully boring."

"Well, then, I'm glad you decided to come along."

"This will be frightfully boring, too," Victoria said with a shrug. "I don't know your father or your sister. But anything is better than being with that old fusspot."

"Victoria, Miss Rutherford may have her drawbacks, but she does care about you."

"Who does she think she is, my mother?" Victoria turned from the TV to face me. Her eyes were red and her lower lip was quivering.

I had never seen her like this. "Victoria?"

"I hate Miss Rutherford! I hate hate *hate* her — all her rules and her loud voice and her frowning little face! And I hate you, too!"

I leaned over and turned off the TV. "Maybe we should talk — "

"Turn that back on!" she commanded. "You're just like her! I hate you, do you understand? George, take me home this minute!"

"Who-o-oa, whoa, it's okay." I moved closer to her. "You know, your mom and dad will be back."

Victoria crossed her arms defiantly and shrank away. "No, they won't! They're going to fly away forever. They hate me! They want to leave me with Miss Rutherford and . . . and *you*, in a strange house until I waste away like an ugly old gnome."

I smiled. "A princess can never be an ugly old gnome, you know. I read it in a book."

I could see Victoria's scowl soften. I lifted my arm and gently put it around her.

Burying her face in my shoulder, she began to sob — huge sobs that made her shoulders rise and fall.

"I know how you must feel," I said. "My dad is on a long trip, too."

"You *don't* know how I feel! At least your father is in this country. At least he comes home and stays there for a long time! At least he's not *always* leaving you."

I gave Victoria a tissue from a small pack I carry in my coat pocket. "I guess you want them to stay put for awhile, huh?"

Victoria nodded. "Forever and ever. I wish they never had to go away on their silly jobs to those silly countries. I absolutely *hate* the United Nations!"

"Victoria, have you told your parents how you feel?" I asked.

"Don't be daft. Of course not. I can't."

"Why not? What do you think will happen?"

Victoria shrugged. "They'll be mad at me. I can't have them mad at me, you know. What if they meet a quiet, nice girl in Brussels or Paris and decide to have her as a daughter?"

Suddenly it all hit me. Sharon had been right. Victoria really was afraid.

"Victoria, do your parents call when they're traveling?"

"Oh, yes."

"And bring you back gifts?"

Victoria brightened a bit. "Last time, they brought that dollhouse. That was from Germany."

"Really? Well, then, they don't forget you when they go away."

"I suppose not. They *are* my parents."

I laughed. "And are they sending a dollhouse to a little girl in Brussels or Paris?"

A tiny smile formed on Victoria's face. "A dollhouse full of brussels sprouts, perhaps."

"Ew. Cooked?"

"Mashed. Mashed and creamed, with mustard!"

"And chocolate chips!"

"Way gross!" Victoria burst into giggles. "Oh, Mary Anne, you simply must visit me after the party. Dolly Wupperton is in such a fix. She has the flu and her parents are away and that wretched boy next door is singing under her window!"

"I'd love to. Why don't we invite Karen over, too? She lives practically next door to you, and she'd love the house."

Smack. Down went the curtain over Victoria's face again.

I wanted to kick myself for opening my big mouth.

"I don't think so," Victoria said. "I don't know her well."

"She's a nice girl. You could invite her over."

"Then I'd have to be her friend. I can't very well have that."

"Why not?"

Victoria rolled her eyes. "I'll only be leaving in six months, remember? If I have friends here, well, what a mess *that* would be."

"But, Victoria, six months is a long time. You can't refuse to make friends, just because you're afraid to lose them. I mean, we all naturally make friends. You'd have to work hard not to."

"Work?"

"Sure. Sooner or later, you're bound to find you actually like a kid or two. And chances are they'll like you, too. What are you going to do — hang a sign around your neck that says 'Go away'?"

Victoria took a deep breath. "Well, no . . ."

"Look. It's hard when people we love go away. And it's hard to move from one place to another. But we can't just roll up like an old carpet and stop living. So you make a few friends, then you leave — that's not so awful. You become pen pals. You see each other on visits. You e-mail each other. Send photos. Long-distance friendships can be fun. I know from experience. My own stepsister moved to California."

Victoria fell silent.

Outside, the low, curved buildings of the airport were coming into view. A small propellor plane was landing to our right.

"Mary Anne," Victoria said in a small voice, "if I invite Karen over, do I have to invite that horrid brother, David Michael?"

I couldn't help laughing. "No. Kristy will take care of him, I'm sure."

Victoria turned back to the window. "Well, I'll think about it."

It was a start. A start was better than nothing.

CHAPTER 15

"Eeeeeeeeee!"

"AAAAAAHHHHH!"

No. That was not the tropical room of the Central Park Zoo. It was the arrivals area of the airport. The *ee* was Dawn. (I'm more an *aah* person.)

"Oh, I'm so tired!" Dawn said. "I couldn't sleep! But I'm so wide awake, you know? And I can't wait to see Mom and I have so much to tell you and *hi*, you must be Queen Victoria — *Princess*! Or whatever! Sorry. I'm Dawn."

Victoria smiled and gave a curtsey. "Charmed."

"I *love* it!" Dawn said. "I mean, pleased to meet you. Oh, I am so spaced out!"

Dawn took a deep breath. Before I could say a word, I saw a familiar figure lumbering toward me from another flight gate.

He did have an ear-to-ear smile, too.

"*Daddy!*" I screamed.

"Richard!" Dawn yelled.

I ran to him and threw my arms around his shoulders. "Well!" he said. "Well, what a nice greeting."

We introduced him to Victoria, then we all went down to the luggage claim area.

Dad's suitcase came around right away. I won't tell you Dawn's reaction to the cardboard case marked *Refrigerated bratwurst handle with care.*

We could not stop talking on the ride home. Even Victoria was caught up in the spirit. When Dad told her Milwaukee had a beach in the city, she said it must be the most fascinating place in the world.

George stopped off at the Kents' to pick up Miss Rutherford. She emerged from the house in heels and a fur-lined coat. "Ah," she said to my dad as she sat in the limo, "I see the apple doesn't fall far from the tree."

Dad looked a little puzzled. "Uh, thank you."

The strength of her perfume seemed to suck up all the oxygen in the limo. My dad's face was turning red. I don't know how we kept from gagging.

George zoomed to our house in record time, probably so we could emerge into the fresh air faster. As we walked up the lawn to our house, George, Dad, Victoria, Miss Rutherford, and I formed a kind of wall in front of Dawn.

Sharon greeted us at the door. "Hi, everybody — oh, and especially you!"

She gave my father a big hug — and came eye-to-eye with Dawn.

"Wha — Daw — how — ohhhhh, my baby!"

Forget it. Her face went completely red. Tears misted her eyes, and a big, big smile lit up her face.

She practically pushed Dad aside. She gave Dawn such a big hug, it lifted her and her suitcase off the porch.

"Hi, Mom," Dawn squeaked.

"Lovely," Miss Rutherford said. She was actually crying. Her mascara was already streaking. Dad was beaming. I was honking into a tissue.

Victoria went running into the house. I followed her to the kitchen. There, Mom's health loaf was still in the making (late, of course). Her other dishes were simmering on the range.

But something was missing, and I wasn't sure what.

"Where's the turkey?" Victoria asked.

That was it. I didn't smell the turkey!

Odd. All Sharon had to do was put it in the oven and . . .

140

Uh-oh.

Quickly I opened the oven. The turkey was in there, all right. It was still cold.

The oven was set to Off.

"Arrggggh . . ." I flicked the knob to Warm. Then I ran inside and whispered the news to Sharon.

She was embarrassed. "Oh, dear. I guess that means we won't eat until two o'clock or so."

"No problem," Dad said. "I can show you all my slides of Milwaukee."

Miss Rutherford's smile froze. "Charming."

"Fine with me!" George said with a shrug.

Victoria tugged on my sleeve. "Do you suppose I could play with Karen while we're waiting?"

"Well, she may visit with Kristy later," I said. "All the BSC members are coming over."

"What if she doesn't?" Victoria asked. "Perhaps George could drive me back with you for an hour or so while Miss Rutherford is watching the slides. Would you come too, Dawn?"

Everyone spoke at once:

"Uh, well, em, er . . ." Miss Rutherford sputtered.

"Sure," Dawn replied, "for awhile, at least."

"But you just got here!" Sharon complained.

"At your service!" George said.

I went to the phone. I could tell Victoria

wanted to flee the slide show, and I didn't blame her. Oh, well, slides or not, I was sure of one thing. It was going to be a great, great holiday.

As I tapped out the number, Victoria waltzed happily around the kitchen. I could hear Dawn laughing out loud, and my dad's voice describing something that had happened to him at the airport.

I smiled. I had a lot to be thankful for.

Dear Reader,

The title for *Mary Anne and the Little Princess* came from one of my favorite books when I was growing up — *A Little Princess* by Frances Hodgson Burnett. Another of my favorite books was also by Frances Burnett — *The Secret Garden*. When I was a kid, I just loved reading. (As an adult, I still do.) I had a lot of favorite books. Among them were the Mary Poppins books, the Wizard of Oz books, the Doctor Doolittle books, Marguerite Henry's horse stories, Roald Dahl's books (especially *James and the Giant Peach*), *Mr. Popper's Penguins*, and *Baby Island*.

My sister and I were very lucky because when we were growing up we were frequently given books as gifts. By the time I was ten, I had a huge shelf full of books I loved. That was why I decided to start a lending library in my bedroom. I spent a long time one summer making pockets to put in the back of each book, and cards to go in the pockets. I opened my library to the kids in the neighborhood, and let them check out books to read. That was the summer I wanted to be a librarian. I changed my mind about a career lots of times after that, but as you can see, I still ended up working with children's books. And I still have all the books that were on the shelves of my long-ago library.

Happy reading,

Ann M. Martin

L. GODWIN

Ann M. Martin

About the Author

ANN MATTHEWS MARTIN was born on August 12, 1955. She grew up in Princeton, NJ, with her parents and her younger sister, Jane.

Although Ann used to be a teacher and then an editor of children's books, she's now a full-time writer. She gets the ideas for her books from many different places. Some are based on personal experiences. Others are based on childhood memories and feelings. Many are written about contemporary problems or events.

All of Ann's characters, even the members of the Baby-sitters Club, are made up. (So is Stoneybrook.) But many of her characters are based on real people. Sometimes Ann names her characters after people she knows, other times she chooses names she likes.

In addition to the Baby-sitters Club books, Ann Martin has written many other books for children. Her favorite is *Ten Kids*, *No Pets* because she loves big families and she loves animals. Her favorite Baby-sitters Club book is *Kristy's Big Day*. (By the way, Kristy is her favorite baby-sitter!)

Ann M. Martin now lives in New York with her cats, Gussie and Woody. Her hobbies are reading, sewing, and needlework — especially making clothes for children.

Notebook Pages

This Baby-sitters Club book belongs to _____ .

I am _____ years old and in the _____

grade.

The name of my school is _____ .

I got this BSC book from _____ .

I started reading it on _____ and

finished reading it on _____ .

The place where I read most of this book is _____ .

My favorite part was when _____ .

If I could change anything in the story, it might be the part when

_____ .

My favorite character in the Baby-sitters Club is _____ .

The BSC member I am most like is _____ .

because _____ .

If I could write a Baby-sitters Club book it would be about ____

_____ .

#102 Mary Anne and the Little Princess

In *Mary Anne and the Little Princess*, a distant heir to the British throne arrives in Stoneybrook. Mary Anne is asked to show her around Stoneybrook and teach her about American culture. If a princess came to my town, I would show her ___ _____. I would teach her how to _____ _____. Mary Anne and her friends teach Victoria words such as "cool" and "great." Some words I would teach her are _____. Some of the questions I would ask Victoria about being a princess are:

_____

_____. If I were a member of the royal family, one rule I would make would be _____ _____. My crown would look like this:

MARY ANNE'S

Party girl -- age 4

Sitting for the Pikes is always an adventure.

Sitting for Andrea and Jenny Prezzioso -- a quiet moment.

SCRAPBOOK

*Logan and me.
Summer luv at Sea City.*

Illustrations by Angelo Tillery

*My family...
Jeff, Dad and Sharon.
Dawn and me. And Tigger.*

Read all the books
about **Mary Anne**
in the Baby-sitters Club series
by Ann M. Martin

Mysteries:

Portrait Collection:

THE BABY-SITTERS CLUB

Look for #103

HAPPY HOLIDAYS, JESSI

It was the first of December. The beginning of the absolute best month of the year.

I don't know about you, but I think the holidays are truly magical. The moment I see the first Christmas decorations in the store windows, I'm a little kid again. I feed Christmas carol recordings into the CD player all day long. Thinking about presents, I'm weak in the knees. And when I look forward to a whole week of Kwanzaa, my eyes water. Honest.

The entire month of December I'm one big tingle.

"Yvonne called today," Mama said to Daddy. "She was wondering what our plans were for the holidays."

I nearly dropped a plate. Yvonne is my aunt. Her daughter, Keisha, is my all-time favorite cousin.

We grew up together in Oakley, New Jersey,

before my branch of the family moved to Stoneybrook. "Can they come over for Christmas?" I asked.

"Yea!" Becca shouted from the family room.

"Well, they're spending Christmas at home," Mama replied, "but they'd love to get together for Kwanzaa — "

"Can they?" I asked. "Oh, please please please please?"

Becca rushed in, clutching an enormous department store catalog. *"Pleeeeeeeease?"*

Daddy laughed. "As long as they bring some pecan pie, they're welcome in this house."

"Then we just have to figure out exactly when," Mama said.

"You're not planning to have them over for the entire week?" Aunt Cecelia called out from the bathroom. "That's an awful lot of work."

"Oh, Cecelia, don't be a Kwanzaa Grinch," Daddy said.

"Bup! Bup! Bup!" shouted Squirt, hopping into the kitchen.

Daddy went running after Squirt. "Maybe not a week," he said over his shoulder. "But a couple of days, at least."

"Definitely for the *karamu* feast," Mama agreed.

"Yeaaa!" I did a little pirouette.

Collect 'em all!

100 (and more)
Reasons to Stay Friends Forever!

More titles... ➧

❑ MG48226-2	#82	Jessi and the Troublemaker		$3.99
❑ MG48235-1	#83	Stacey vs. the BSC		$3.50
❑ MG48228-9	#84	Dawn and the School Spirit War		$3.50
❑ MG48236-X	#85	Claudi Kishi, Live from WSTO		$3.50
❑ MG48227-0	#86	Mary Anne and Camp BSC		$3.50
❑ MG48237-8	#87	Stacey and the Bad Girls	＼	$3.50
❑ MG22872-2	#88	Farewell, Dawn		$3.50
❑ MG22873-0	#89	Kristy and the Dirty Diapers		$3.50
❑ MG22874-9	#90	Welcome to the BSC, Abby		$3.99
❑ MG22875-1	#91	Claudia and the First Thanksgiving		$3.50
❑ MG22876-5	#92	Mallory's Christmas Wish		$3.50
❑ MG22877-3	#93	Mary Anne and the Memory Garden		$3.99
❑ MG22878-1	#94	Stacey McGill, Super Sitter		$3.99
❑ MG22879-X	#95	Kristy + Bart = ?		$3.99
❑ MG22880-3	#96	Abby's Lucky Thirteen		$3.99
❑ MG22881-1	#97	Claudia and the World's Cutest Baby		$3.99
❑ MG22882-X	#98	Dawn and Too Many Sitters		$3.99
❑ MG69205-4	#99	Stacey's Broken Heart		$3.99
❑ MG69206-2	#100	Kristy's Worst Idea		$3.99
❑ MG69207-0	#101	Claudia Kishi, Middle School Dropout		$3.99
❑ MG69208-9	#102	Mary Anne and the Little Princess		$3.99
❑ MG69209-7	#103	Happy Holidays, Jessi		$3.99
❑ MG45575-3		Logan's Story Special Edition Readers' Request		$3.25
❑ MG47118-X		Logan Bruno, Boy Baby-sitter		
		Special Edition Readers' Request		$3.50
❑ MG47756-0		Shannon's Story Special Edition		$3.50
❑ MG47686-6		The Baby-sitters Club Guide to Baby-sitting		$3.25
❑ MG47314-X		The Baby-sitters Club Trivia and Puzzle Fun Book		$2.50
❑ MG48400-1		BSC Portrait Collection: Claudia's Book		$3.50
❑ MG22864-1		BSC Portrait Collection: Dawn's Book		$3.50
❑ MG69181-3		BSC Portrait Collection: Kristy's Book		$3.99
❑ MG22865-X		BSC Portrait Collection: Mary Anne's Book		$3.99
❑ MG48399-4		BSC Portrait Collection: Stacey's Book		$3.50
❑ MG92713-2		The Complete Guide to The Baby-sitters Club		$4.95
❑ MG47151-1		The Baby-sitters Club Chain Letter		$14.95
❑ MG48295-5		The Baby-sitters Club Secret Santa		$14.95
❑ MG45074-3		The Baby-sitters Club Notebook		$2.50
❑ MG44783-1		The Baby-sitters Club Postcard Book		$4.95

Available wherever you buy books...or use this order form.

Scholastic Inc., P.O. Box 7502, 2931 E. McCarty Street, Jefferson City, MO 65102

Please send me the books I have checked above. I am enclosing $_____
(please add $2.00 to cover shipping and handling). Send check or money order—
no cash or C.O.D.s please.

Name_____ Birthdate_____

Address _____

City_____ State/Zip _____

BSC5962

THE BABY-SITTERS CLUB®

by Ann M. Martin

Collect and read these exciting BSC Super Specials, Mysteries, and Super Mysteries along with your favorite Baby-sitters Club books!

BSC Super Specials

❏ BBK44240-6	Baby-sitters on Board! Super Special #1	$3.95
❏ BBK44239-2	Baby-sitters' Summer Vacation Super Special #2	$3.95
❏ BBK43973-1	Baby-sitters' Winter Vacation Super Special #3	$3.95
❏ BBK42493-9	Baby-sitters' Island Adventure Super Special #4	$3.95
❏ BBK43575-2	California Girls! Super Special #5	$3.95
❏ BBK43576-0	New York, New York! Super Special #6	$4.50
❏ BBK44963-X	Snowbound! Super Special #7	$3.95
❏ BBK44962-X	Baby-sitters at Shadow Lake Super Special #8	$3.95
❏ BBK45661-X	Starring The Baby-sitters Club! Super Special #9	$3.95
❏ BBK45674-1	Sea City, Here We Come! Super Special #10	$3.95
❏ BBK47015-9	The Baby-sitters Remember Super Special #11	$3.95
❏ BBK48308-0	Here Come the Bridesmaids! Super Special #12	$3.95
❏ BBK22883-8	Aloha, Baby-sitters! Super Special #13	$4.50

BSC Mysteries

❏ BAI44084-5	#1 Stacey and the Missing Ring	$3.50
❏ BAI44085-3	#2 Beware, Dawn!	$3.50
❏ BAI44799-8	#3 Mallory and the Ghost Cat	$3.50
❏ BAI44800-5	#4 Kristy and the Missing Child	$3.50
❏ BAI44801-3	#5 Mary Anne and the Secret in the Attic	$3.50
❏ BAI44961-3	#6 The Mystery at Claudia's House	$3.50
❏ BAI44960-5	#7 Dawn and the Disappearing Dogs	$3.50
❏ BAI44959-1	#8 Jessi and the Jewel Thieves	$3.50
❏ BAI44958-3	#9 Kristy and the Haunted Mansion	$3.50
❏ BAI45696-2	#10 Stacey and the Mystery Money	$3.50

More titles ➡

The Baby-sitters Club books continued...

❏ BAI47049-3	#11 Claudia and the Mystery at the Museum	$3.50
❏ BAI47050-7	#12 Dawn and the Surfer Ghost	$3.50
❏ BAI47051-5	#13 Mary Anne and the Library Mystery	$3.50
❏ BAI47052-3	#14 Stacey and the Mystery at the Mall	$3.50
❏ BAI47053-1	#15 Kristy and the Vampires	$3.50
❏ BAI47054-X	#16 Claudia and the Clue in the Photograph	$3.99
❏ BAI48232-7	#17 Dawn and the Halloween Mystery	$3.50
❏ BAI48233-5	#18 Stacey and the Mystery at the Empty House	$3.50
❏ BAI48234-3	#19 Kristy and the Missing Fortune	$3.50
❏ BAI48309-9	#20 Mary Anne and the Zoo Mystery	$3.50
❏ BAI48310-2	#21 Claudia and the Recipe for Danger	$3.50
❏ BAI22866-8	#22 Stacey and the Haunted Masquerade	$3.50
❏ BAI22867-6	#23 Abby and the Secret Society	$3.99
❏ BAI22868-4	#24 Mary Anne and the Silent Witness	$3.99
❏ BAI22869-2	#25 Kristy and the Middle School Vandal	$3.99
❏ BAI22870-6	#26 Dawn Schafer, Undercover Baby-sitter	$3.99

BSC Super Mysteries

❏ BAI48311-0	The Baby-sitters' Haunted House Super Mystery #1	$3.99
❏ BAI22871-4	Baby-sitters Beware Super Mystery #2	$3.99
❏ BAI69180-5	Baby-sitters' Fright Night Super Mystery #3	$4.50

Want to find out what it's like to be a member of the BSC?

JOIN THE CLUB.

━━ Friendship Kit ━━

NOW ON CD-ROM FOR PC & MAC!

You'll feel like the newest member of The Baby-sitters Club, when you join Kristy, Claudia, and the rest of the girls to use your creativity and imagination every day! With The BSC Friendship Kit, you can create, use, and send lots of cool stuff, including:

- Stationery
- Calendar
- Bulletin Board
- Address Book
- Games

- Posters
- Baby-sitting Forms
- Secret Messages
- Virtual Mail
- Diary

- Greeting Cards
- Tickets
- Savings Bank

 **PHILIPS**
http://www.philipsfamily.com

- -

To find out more about The BSC Friendship Kit visit your local retailer or fill out this coupon and mail to:
**Philips Media, 10960 Wilshire Blvd.,
7th floor, Los Angeles, CA 90024, Attn: BSC Friendship Kit.**

Please Print:

Name_____ Birthdate___/___/___
　　　　First　　　　　Last　　　　　　　　　　　　M　D　Y

Address_____

City_____ State_____ Zip_____

Telephone (____)_____ Boy ❏ Girl ❏

PHIL596